Title

en ma fin gît ma commencement
(in my end is my beginning)
Motto of Mary Queen of Scots.

Copyright and Disclaimer

First Published 2022.

Copyright © Sean T. Rassleagh, 2022.

The moral right of Sean T. Rassleagh to be identified as the author of this work has been asserted.

The Repository Suppository is a work of fiction. The novel is set many years in the future in Edinburgh's Old Town and some scenes are set in historic buildings. No connection between the fictional occupiers of premises in the novel and the present or previous occupiers of premises in real life is intended or should be inferred.

All rights reserved.

Cover design by Rafael Andres.

Milton Mowbray

Edinburgh, August 2046.

James Miranda Fergusson was heading for his PhD viva, and he was nervous. He'd already submitted twice and been knocked back with major revisions on both occasions. Under university rules, this was his last chance. Fortunately, he was sure there wouldn't be a problem with the latest revision of his thesis since his supervisor, Dr Knox, had decided it was less trouble to write the new draft herself than correct his work. He hadn't understood most of what she'd written, but in his view that was a good sign that it was PhD level. The thing that made him nervous was that he'd have to defend it. Dr Knox had given him a set of PowerPoint slides with extensive notes, so the presentation element should be fine, but what if the external examiner had questions? According to the student union handbook, the best approach in those circumstances was to feign outrage at some remark of the examiner followed by storming out and lodging a claim of discrimination. He hoped it wouldn't come to that, but realistically, it probably would.

The meeting room was near the top of the Informatics Department building on Potterrow and had an expansive view over the Central Mosque towards Arthur's Seat. James arrived with two minutes to spare. The external examiner was already in the room, chatting to Dr Knox and the university's internal examiner, who were both attending by video link. It wasn't surprising that Dr Knox could not attend in person since she had been euthanised several years ago and her consciousness uploaded to the cloud. James's best guess was that her neural network currently resided on a computer in a Guild space station somewhere near Mars. He was more surprised that the internal examiner had chosen to attend by video link from his home office. The lazy bastard was probably intending to have his computer synthesise his image on the link while he played a game. Or, at least, that's what James would have done in his place. But all to the good, the less attention the examiners paid, the better.

The internal examiner called the meeting to order, said something about the fire escape route and offered to have one of the robot servitors deliver coffee and biscuits. Then it was time for James's presentation. He stood up and told the computer to bring up his first slide. He had a lot of slides and gameplay footage illustrating his use of experimental MedChip Corporation sensors to interface a human brain to 'Red Lead Redaction', a commercial video game about lawyers in the Wild West. The game was the latest installment in a long running franchise and most of the more exciting career options had already been explored. Dr Knox had prudently provided enough material for him to talk continuously for the entire three hours allotted to the Viva. The more he talked, the less time there would be for questions.

James finished his introduction with thanks to his supervisor and commercial sponsors and moved on to discuss the video game his software would interface to. This provided an excellent opportunity to spend ten minutes showing the titles and loading screen.

The external examiner perked up. James guessed he was around sixty-five, but well preserved. He was thin, of average height, and his white hair was clipped short. Since the university was paying for his time, the examiner had decided the occasion merited wearing a formal shirt with a collar under his faded sweatshirt. The sweatshirt, the front of which read 'wasted!' in Polaris Games' trademark font, served the dual purpose of confirming his credentials and covering the formal shirt sufficiently that there was no need to iron it or wear a tie.

"I worked on that game, you know," he announced, "I was with the company for thirty years, doing artificial intelligence code for the Non-Player Characters."

"Oh shit, a fucking expert!" thought James, but he controlled himself and said, "I'm so honoured to have one of the game developers as an examiner."

"Yeah, I did some work on the horses in that one, got an award for it. But mostly I was on the Taking and Driving Away franchise. That earned billions for the company. Not that I saw much of it."

Dr Knox knew she wasn't supposed to talk during the viva since she was the supervisor, but this was exactly what she'd intended would happen and it needed to be encouraged.

"I'd be so interested to learn about the history of the games. Perhaps you could tell us more?"

But the internal examiner was having none of it. "We may have time for that after James finishes his presentation, Dr Knox."

"Of course, of course, I'm forgetting myself. Please carry on, James."

Ten minutes later, around about slide five, James noticed the external examiner's eyes flicker closed for a few seconds before he woke again with a start. As he approached slide fifty, the examiner slumped forward in his chair.

"Cushion!" hissed Dr Knox. "There's one on the chair next to you. Put it on the table in front of him, quick. Before he bangs his head."

James got the external examiner comfortably snoozing and carried on with his presentation. The internal examiner seemed completely oblivious to what was happening. Most likely, he was playing Frogger. He looked like someone who would play Frogger or Candy Crush.

With ten minutes of the three hours allotted to the Viva remaining, James had got to slide one hundred and fifty-three.

Dr Knox cut in again. "Thank you, James, but I am conscious of the time. Perhaps we should end it there to allow some time for questions. ANTHONY WHAT DO YOU THINK?" She almost shouted the last sentence.

"Mmm. Hunhh." The external examiner was waking up.

"I was just saying there are only ten minutes left. Perhaps we should end the presentation, fascinating though it has been, to allow some time for questions?"

"Oh, yes, excellent presentation, James, very impressive work."

"Do you have any questions, Anthony?"

"Yes. I was wondering if this neural interfacing technique could also be applied to the Taking and Driving Away game. I'd love to see that done. Do you foresee any difficulties?"

"Well, obviously the codebases are now running on the same graphics platform, so in terms of visual immersion I would see no obstacles to that. Of course, there is a wide range of vehicles in the TDA franchise so some development would be needed and the neural interfacing would provide a first-person experience where

TDA is normally played in third-person, but I think it is certainly feasible."

The internal examiner had also noticed the time, paused his game, and returned his attention to the meeting.

"Thank you, James. Very impressive defence. Unfortunately, we only have five minutes remaining and I have another meeting scheduled, so perhaps you can continue this discussion with Dr Merchant offline. Would you leave the room now so the examiners can have a confidential discussion?"

Four minutes and thirty seconds later, they called James back and told him he'd passed with no amendments required. The video screens clicked off, and James and the external examiner were left alone in the room. They stood up and began to collect their things.

"It's been very nice meeting you, James. You know, in my day after these things, there was usually a bit of a celebration. A meal or a few drinks in the pub with the supervisor and examiners. Videoconferencing is all very efficient, but it takes away the social element. Are you going out to celebrate with your friends?"

James shook his head as they headed for the door.

"I don't have many friends in real life. I have lots of online friends from gaming."

"I was wondering if I could get a demo of your system. I worked on TDA for decades. It would be amazing to play it through a neural interface, completely immersed in the map as if you were in Los Espíritus."

Neither of them was a great fan of stairs, so when they reached the end of the corridor they waited for the lift.

"Unfortunately, I wasn't allowed to keep a copy of my code. You know... because of the developers of the neural interfacing chip I was using."

"Dr Knox and MedChip. Enough said. Best not to say the G-word."

"I didn't say the G-word."

"No, of course not. Nobody said it. But we can still talk about the game. I bet you know your way around the map almost as well as I do after a seven-year PhD. What's it like being immersed in it at the neural level?"

"I'm afraid I don't know. You'd need to ask Dr Knox. The procedure to allow neural immersion is not reversible. Personally, I'd be too scared to have it done."

"To be honest, I was more than a little surprised when Dr Knox contacted me about being the external examiner for your thesis. I still remember the meal at their leaving party when she and her husband were euthanised, absolutely delicious. And now she's on a video link…"

Dr Merchant suddenly understood what had happened to Dr Knox.

"Oh God, that's what you meant by 'not reversible'. I always assumed she had a fatal disease, but she was euthanised because the process to upload her neural network couldn't be done on a live person."

They emerged into the lobby, and James reached out to push open the main door. As he did so, the sleeve of his sweatshirt moved back over his wrist and Dr Merchant saw the shiny black bracelet on his left wrist.

"I hope you don't mind me asking, but that's a Brothel bracelet, isn't it"?

"Yeah, I got a conviction for unhealthy eating a couple of years back and they tagged me for a week after my caning. I kept the bracelet because the Fuel you get when you are registered with the Brothel tastes so much better than the normal stuff."

"Most young people seem to have them now. It's sad, in my day people could pay off their university loans from their salary."

"These days almost everybody has advanced degrees and hardly anybody has a job. The Brothel is about all there is when you are young and need money, that and being a servant or the new City Farm if you're really desperate." James shuddered at the thought.

"Tell you what, I'd like to get your opinion on something I've been working on since I left Polaris. Would you be interested?"

"Sure!"

"The only thing is, it is highly confidential. Since you're a Brothel employee, the easiest thing would be for me to hire you as an escort, so you are bound by their Non-Disclosure Agreement and paid for your time."

"You really only want to talk about your new project?" asked James skeptically.

Anthony smiled, "Don't worry. I'm only paying for your time, so if something clever comes out of the discussion, I will own it. I can afford five hundred euros to buy half a day from the Brothel, but I can't afford a couple of thousand to get a lawyer to draft a bulletproof contract."

"That's fair enough, as long as we are clear."

Anthony got out his phone and made the booking using the Brothel app, four hours starting immediately.

— ♦ —

"The computers are at my place; I just live around the corner in QuarterMile," said Dr Merchant, "but why don't we pick up something to eat first? It's been ages since I had fish and chips."

It was a rare treat to have actual fish with brown sauce: even the fish-and-chips flavoured Brothel Fuel was not a patch on the chip shop, so James readily agreed. They walked through the University campus and past Old College towards North Bridge, retracing the path James had taken on the way to his viva. But now he was James Miranda Fergusson PhD. Doctor Fergusson. Well, not quite yet, since he still needed to graduate, but as good as.

On South Bridge they went past a dilapidated amusement arcade. It had been there for as long as James could remember. He always peeked in as he walked past and daydreamed about what he would do if he owned the place. But today the door was padlocked, the windows were whitewashed and there was an estate agent's sign nailed above it. It appeared as if the lack of customers had finally caught up with it.

"I read on Facebook that this arcade was the inspiration for the one in TDA," said James, "that one of the game's writers saw it and got the idea. It's a shame it's closed."

"I never heard that when I was working for the company," said Anthony, "but it's close enough to our office that I suppose it is possible."

"I bet it doesn't have a secret underground headquarters like in the game," James joked.

"I wouldn't be so sure," said Anthony. "South Bridge and Alex Salmond Bridge look like normal streets, but they are actually bridges. The unusual thing is they have buildings on either side, right up against the bridge, turning the space underneath a bridge arch into a closed-off vault. In theory, if you owned that arcade, and you could get one, maybe two, stories down from the street level and make an opening, you could access that hidden space and have an underground headquarters."

"Do you think it's possible to get into the vault under the bridge from the arcade?"

"Years ago, one of the walking tour companies used to take groups into the vaults under the bridge. There is a way in somewhere, probably not from the arcade, though."

"You know," said James, "if I had the money, I'd buy the arcade and put in Virtual Reality equipment like in the place on Victoria Street. I'd map the VR zone to the upstairs area of the arcade in TDA. I reckon an amusement arcade with a bar could attract a lot of tourists by saying it was the inspiration for the one in TDA."

"I don't see why not. If cafes can get business by claiming an association with the wizard books, why wouldn't it work for an arcade and TDA?"

They continued walking along South Bridge and turned right onto the Royal Mile. The chip shop was further down, near the parliament. They ate in silence on the way back until the chips ran out just as they got to the end of Chambers Street, near the statue of Greyfriars' Bobby.

"There's one thing I'd like to ask, if you're not allowed to tell me that's OK, but I'm curious."

"What's that?"

"How come you guys never finished TDA 6. I mean, TDA 5 came out in 2010."

"2013."

"OK 2013, but it's now 2046 and you're still selling TDA 5. I mean, there's been a lot of great new content in DLCs but it's still the same old game. Why couldn't you get TDA 6 to work?"

There was a pause before Anthony replied.

"Well, seeing as anything I say is covered by the Brothel's NDA, I guess I can tell you."

"You don't need to worry about me saying anything. That NDA terrifies me!"

"TDA 6 wasn't an easy project. Polaris had more than a thousand developers on it for maybe 15 years. Also, we needed the internet and graphics chips to get significantly more powerful before our vision would be practical on low-cost PCs and consoles. But in the end, we finished it."

"You finished TDA 6!"

"Sure. It would be about ten years ago. Not long before I got fired from the company. We finished it, we tested it and before it went live on the TDA Online servers, we sent the master copy of the source code to the National Library of Scotland."

"Why would you do that?"

"It's the copyright library for Scotland. It's actually the law that they have to get a copy of every publication. More to the point, if you give them a copy and they log it into their collection, then you can easily prove the date on your copyright claim, which avoids a lot of argument if you have to go to court."

"OK, so you e-mailed them the source code."

"No, the library only deals with physical media. We were lucky they didn't insist it was printed out on paper! We bought sixteen of the newest 256 Terabyte flash drives and filled them all. It was a lot of data: the full repositories, not just the final version of the code but a complete log of every change and addition made during the development, so any copyright case would be bulletproof. Then we put the flash drives in a custom-designed metal case and delivered them to the library in an armoured truck. The source code was our crown jewels; TDA 5 was bringing in two billion dollars a year."

"So, if it was finished, how come nobody is playing TDA 6? There must be hundreds of thousands of people that play TDA Online and they're all waiting for the new one!"

"The problem was that the Greens held the justice minister post in the coalition government when the game was finished," Anthony said bitterly, "the Greens hate everything about TDA: fast cars, guns, planes and questionable jokes. They'd already got their Politically Correct Speech Act through the Holyrood parliament, but we thought we were OK because acts of parliament do not become law until the King signs them and they don't apply retrospectively. The signing is supposed to happen in a scheduled ceremony for all the laws passed in the parliamentary session. However, the justice minister personally took the law across to the palace and got the King's signature as soon as she heard we had delivered the game to the library."

"What a bitch!" said James. "I could have been playing TDA 6 for ten years! I can't believe I gave the Greens my second vote!"

"If the King had signed the law when it was supposed to be signed, we would have been in the clear to distribute the game and everyone would be playing it. As it was, the Political Correctness Division of Police Scotland sent their elite Pronoun Enforcement Squad to raid our office the day after we lodged the source code in the National Library. When they saw the new game they charged us with 128 counts of sexism, glorification of violence, depicting a firearm, incitement to cause carbon pollution, incitement to manually drive a motor vehicle, incitement to robbery and a bunch of other things. If it had gone to court and we had lost, everyone involved would have been working the fines off in the Brothel for the rest of their lives. I'd have been lucky to escape with my balls."

"But the company could still have released the game outside of Scotland?"

"Maybe in America, because of the First Amendment. We wouldn't be able to distribute it in the EU if a Scottish court ruled against us. We could have released it in England, of course; international law doesn't apply there, but it doesn't make any difference because there are no computers in England. Fortunately for my testicles, the justice minister had forgotten one important detail: they raided us before we had distributed any copies to the public, and the procurer fiscal couldn't actually charge us with anything until we did. In the end, it was resolved with a private meeting in the justice minister's office: we agreed to delete all copies of the game materials, they agreed there would be no public statements about the case, we made a small political contribution and that was it. Thousands of man-years of development written off. The developers were completely dispirited and with TDA 6 cancelled there was nothing to work on, so the company made most of us redundant."

"So that's it, TDA 6 was deleted. It's never going to appear. All the posts and rumours on Facebook and YouTube about it coming out in 2050 are just nonsense?" asked James.

"There's only one copy of TDA 6 in existence, the one we delivered to the National Library of Scotland. It was placed in the restricted section of the library in the high-security vault under their building on Alex Salmond Bridge. A few years ago, the library's budget was cut and the above-ground section of that building was taken over by the Historic Crimes and Grievances Division of Police Scotland."

"So, it's in an underground vault, carved out of rock, with a police station on top of it?"

"Not just any rock. Edinburgh is built over a series of ancient volcanos. The castle crag, Arthur's Seat, Calton Hill, Salisbury Crags are all the remains of volcanos. The rock under the library is solidified lava. Igneous rocks like that are far harder and more difficult to tunnel through than the sedimentary rocks you'd find under cities like London. The rocks under Edinburgh today are the ones that withstood being scoured by an ice sheet for hundreds of years."

— ♦ —

They walked through the University Campus and across Middle Meadow Walk to QuarterMile. Anthony had a penthouse flat in one of the glass-and-steel modern blocks. It was deceptively small, just a lounge with a kitchen area and two bedrooms. Most of the floor space was given over to the lounge, which had impressive views over the Meadows through floor to ceiling windows. The walls were decorated with framed posters of the cover artwork from games he had worked. One side of the room was given over to computing equipment: there was a brand-new PC with a full virtual reality set-up, a software development workstation with multiple monitors, and in the corner an old gaming PC from the days when people thought glowing LEDs and a surfeit of fans were cool.

Dr Merchant pointed at the PC in the corner. "That PC over there, the old one, I got it from the leaving-do when your supervisor and her husband were euthanised. They gave all their stuff away; I think it belonged to Dr Knox's husband. It's old, but it is still powerful enough to play TDA. I can use the newer one and we can go into the game together later. Hold on, I'll get some drinks."

He busied himself with making two gin and tonics while James admired his artwork and collection of sci-fi memorabilia. In the place of honour on the back wall of the lounge between cover art posters for TDA 4 and TDA 5 a display case was mounted to the wall. James couldn't believe what was inside.

"Dr Merchant..." James began.

"Call me Anthony!" he replied, handing James his drink.

"Is that a real Mark 2 Phaser?"

"Yes, that's Sulu's phaser. It's a genuine prop from the original series of Star Trek."

"Wow!" James brushed a fingertip against the glass case protecting the precious artifact.

"It was ridiculously expensive, but when I saw it on the auction website I just had to have it."

They took their drinks and went to sit in the lounge.

"So, that thing I told you about TDA 6, it's an enormous secret, you should see the compromise agreement they made me sign when I left the company. Really, don't tell anyone."

"Of course not. You can trust me. And anyway, as you said, I am bound by the Brothel's NDA. If I tell a customer's secrets, my arse is on the line!"

"Since I'm trusting you, maybe you could trust me with a secret, too. I want to know about Dr Knox and her husband, Professor Hume. How can she still be alive? And is the Professor alive too?"

"Well, this is about the G..."

"Don't say it. It may be a trigger word for automated listening devices."

"I think it's safer now that they've left, but you're right, it's best not to say it. They know how to move a person's consciousness from their brain into a computer. But it is a difficult and dangerous process."

"So, what do they do?"

"Well, first the person's head is cut off. They do it carefully, so the nerves and blood vessels are neatly severed and easy to work with. Once the head is separated from the body, it is prepared. The skull is removed to expose the brain, tubes are hooked up to supply it with nutrients, the nerves from the eyes, ears and spinal column are connected to an electrical interface and it is transferred to a plastic capsule for transport."

"Jesus, James! How could you do something like that?"

"I didn't do any of that! I only saw Dr Knox's brain after it was already in the capsule. My job was moving the encapsulated brains to a rack in a secret facility where they were connected to a computer. They were given a simulated environment through the visual and auditory nerves. Over a period of weeks, carbon nanotube connections were grown deep into the brain connecting neurons in the brain to circuits in the computer which implement neural networks electronically. The original organic neurons were slowly dying and, as they did so, the brain adapted to make use of the new electronic neurons. Neurons dying and being replaced is a natural function of a living brain. Over time, more and more of the brain's neural function moved to the electronic neural network on the computer. When enough of it had moved, I removed the head from the rack and the consciousness lived entirely within the computer."

"So, she's living in a simulation?"

"Yes, that's where my work with the Wild West game came in. When people were uploaded, I put them in a small cabin out in the desert in an inaccessible part of the map. Dr Knox paid me to log into the game and help them acclimatise. Then one day they'd all gone, and the cabin was empty."

"What about her husband?"

"I never met the Professor either in real life or in the game. It's strange that I didn't see him if they uploaded him. Mostly, I ran errands for Dr Knox and wrote some of the code she needed to interface her uploaded neural net to the game. They stopped asking me to move heads for them quite a while ago. My guess is they have a new way of uploading people to the cloud."

Anthony checked the time on his phone.

"I've only got an hour left before the booking ends and we won't be covered by NDA after that, so let's get down to business. How would you like to see what I've been working on since I got kicked out of Polaris Games?"

"Sure!"

They went through to the lounge and Anthony pointed at the old computer in the corner of the room.

"That's the computer I picked up from Dr Knox's house at their leaving party. They let the guests take the stuff in their house since they didn't have family to leave it to. Fire it up and have a look."

James touched the mouse, and the screen lit up immediately. It was running TDA Online. Anthony's character had spawned on a camp bed in a rough concrete room.

"That's the underground part of the arcade."

"Yeah. Now go upstairs to the office."

James went up the familiar rocky passage to the manager's office. Even though he spent far more time playing the Western game, he was no stranger to TDA Online.

Sitting in the manager's chair, using the laptop, was a small balding man with glasses. A cane lay propped against the desk beside him.

The man glanced up.

"Hello Anthony!" he said.

James looked around for the keyboard.

"I added voice recognition. You can talk to him," said Anthony.

"I'm not Anthony. I'm just using his character. My name is James," said James.

"Hello, James. Are you a friend of Anthony? I'm Milton. Milton Mowbray."

"You look like…"

"I know. Everybody says that. And they're not far off. Only a few miles." Mr Mowbray chuckled.

James called up the TDA menu to have a look at Milton's stats.

"Level 7,999. K/D 200. 2 trillion TDA dollars and change. Congratulations, you've got a menu!"

"Wrong. I am completely legit. I've been living in this game for ten years."

"Well, Mr Mowbray, you certainly pass the Turing test. You're either a brilliant piece of software or a person is playing your character."

Anthony laughed.

"Yeah, that was the original idea. When I was working on Artificial Intelligence for Non-Player Characters in TDA 6, I wanted to do something like an ELIZA program so the NPCs could respond to simple questions. But then I got fired, and I got my hands on Professor Hume's old games machine. There are three very unusual coprocessors in this PC. Some kind of custom chip and it implements neural networks better than anything I've ever seen. There's nothing programmed about Milton. He's an evolved neural network. It's taken a lot of generations to get to this point and more computing power than even the Professor's accelerator cards could supply for the training. I wrote a menu program for TDA which runs his evolutionary algorithm in the background and gave it away for free. I have a hundred thousand TDA players using my menu to cheat the game most days and they're all providing computer time to help Mr Mowbray here become more intelligent. He's completely autonomous, the most skilled player I know in TDA. He can also access the internet in the real world through the laptops in the game."

"You're telling me you have created artificial life!"

"Not really. I didn't create it, it evolved by itself. I have no idea how a pattern of artificial neurons becomes conscious. A lot of the basic platform code I took from the Professor's original experiment, aside from improving the code to interface the neural network to the game my contribution was stealing sufficient processor power from all those TDA players and being patient enough to let the evolutionary algorithm run for years. The frustrating thing is I can't go public about Milton, because he runs on these special boards from the Professor, and I don't want the… you know who… chopping my head off. Or my former employer suing me for the trade secrets I used to write the menu program. It's good to finally share my project with someone who can understand what's involved in interfacing a neural network to the game and has to keep their mouth shut!"

— ♦ —

After the four-hour appointment ended, James left and Anthony flicked on his TV. He was a fan of the docuseries produced by the Historical Crimes and Grievances Court and today was the finale of their latest case, 'The Crimes of Henry Dundas'. In the previous episode, the procurer fiscal had led an excoriating summing up for the prosecution in which he charged Dundas with unionism, abetting the slave trade, colonialism, theft of public funds and being a Tory. Naturally, he had demanded the death penalty. The defence was lamentably weak and given the lavish production values of the five episodes of dramatised prosecution evidence, the jury felt able to return a guilty verdict on all counts without further deliberation.

The innovative aspect of the current case was that instead of a living relative of Dundas being summoned to face charges in place of their ancestor, the prosecution had subpoenaed his statue. The case had gone to appeal, which had resulted in a delay to the filming schedule, but the Supreme Court unanimously concurred with an erudite analysis by its expert on historical crimes, Baroness McPherson, and ruled that stone likenesses fell within the scope of the Historical Crimes Act and were eligible for criminal sanctions.

Anthony put down his coffee, absorbed by the scene as Sheriff Cockburn straightened his judicial robe, cleared his throat and placed the black cap over his powdered wig. There was immediate silence in the packed courtroom. The camera zoomed in for a close-up as the sentence was pronounced.

"Statue of Henry Dundas, this has been one of the most egregious catalogues of crimes that it has ever been my misfortune to have brought before me! Only one punishment is possible."

The sheriff paused for effect.

"It is the sentence of this court that you shall be wired with explosives by a duly appointed specialist contractor and on the stroke of five o'clock this day, you shall be blown to smithereens!"

"Bailiff, take him down!"

The bailiff placed his hand over a large red button and turned to face the TV camera.

"Ten!" he announced.

The TV channel cut away to show the scene in St Andrew Square where Dundas stood gazing imperiously from his column over the crowd which had gathered on neighbouring streets, kept back at a safe distance by barriers.

A live stream of the bailiff counting down was projected on a thirty-metre high screen for the benefit of the spectators, who were chanting along with the countdown.

"Nine!"

"Eight!"

"Seven!"

Water hoses began to spray the area near the statue.

"Six!"

The TV announcer interjected, sotto voce, "Safety officer has given clearance to enter final countdown."

"Five!"

"Four"

"Detonator circuits armed."

"Three"

"Two"

"One"

As the countdown reached zero, flashes from the explosives rippled up the column and a split second later, a larger charge blew the statue at the top into a million pieces. The whole assemblage collapsed in a carefully planned heap of rubble. A cloud of dust rose from the debris despite the best efforts of the water hoses to damp it down.

The crowd cheered. Fireworks whizzed into the sky and blue and white lasers projected a St Andrew's Cross above the square while the TV screen showed an artist's impression of the new monument commissioned by the council to replace Dundas. Finally, St Andrew would take his rightful place in the centre of St Andrew Square.

Sitting in his comfortable armchair at home only a mile or so from the events on his TV, Anthony heard the bang and felt the building tremble slightly as the charges went off and tons of stonework crashed to the ground. It was by far the most impressive season finale since the public execution of Archibald Campbell for his ancestors' involvement in the massacre of Glencoe.

James was walking down South Bridge on his way home and had just reached the junction with the Royal Mile when the statue fell. The celebratory fireworks and light-show illuminated the sky in front of him and brought a lump to his throat. He did not know what they were in honour of, but it felt as if the city itself was celebrating the award of his PhD.

Sheriff Cockburn also had a lump in his throat as he watched the light-show and fireworks marking the demise of Dundas's statue from the window of his chambers. It was a high point of his career, but he felt it should also be a stepping stone towards greater things. The First Minister had nominated Baroness McPherson to take Scotland's seat on the European Court, leaving a vacancy on the Supreme Court for a justice who specialised in historical crimes and grievances. The paperwork to apply for the position was already filled out and waiting on his computer. Carpe Diem.

The Lawyers

The following morning, Sheriff Cockburn picked up his antique red leather case and crossed the cobbled courtyard in front of St Giles to the Signet Library as he had done almost every Friday morning for the last five years. From there, he made his way through the labyrinthine court buildings to a corridor two floors below street level. Technically, this was part of the detention area, but the floor was plushly carpeted, the doors were of heavy polished wood rather than steel and, unlike most prison cells, the door of the room the Sheriff entered locked from the inside. This secluded section of the historic court buildings dated from the 1800s and was intended for the confinement and punishment of the aristocracy.

Baroness McPherson was waiting nervously when the Sheriff came in and set down his case. She was in her fifties now, but time had been kind to her because, unlike many well-off people, she rarely supplemented the Fuel supplied by the government with richer foods. The composition of Fuel was individually customised to provide the exact nutrients and medication a person required based on measurements from the MedChip implanted in their body, analysis of their DNA, and their age and medical history.

"Good Morning, Marion," said the Sheriff.

It was not usual for a mere Sheriff to address Supreme Court Justice Lady Marion McPherson, Baroness of Leith and Dame Fellatrix of the Kingdom of Scotland by her first name, but this was not a normal meeting.

"Good Morning, Sheriff Cockburn," replied Baroness McPherson.

"Now then," the Sheriff opened his case and took out a printed sheet of A4 paper. The paper was old, and the printing had faded slightly. The Sheriff could have read the sentence from the screen of his phone but he loved old documents.

"Marion McPherson you were convicted of criminal negligence in your handling of the case of Jane Briswell vs the Crown, docket number 28/145271, as a result of which the said Jane Briswell was sentenced to a fine of 200,000 euros to be collected by His Majesty's Brothel. At the point where her conviction was quashed, 150,000 euros of sex work had already been carried out by Ms Briswell."

"Yes, sir."

"In consequence of this and considering the victim impact statement submitted by Ms Briswell, it was stipulated all the services and punishments from each week of Ms Briswell's brothel record would be applied in the corresponding week of your own sentence…"

The Sheriff looked up, waiting for a response.

"Yes, sir."

He glanced down at the sheet. It was a record of Ms Briswell's activities for the Brothel in the third week of August 2035.

"Well, I'm afraid Ms Briswell had quite a busy week. Besides her duties, she was reported for a uniform infraction and swearing at one of the guards, so there is more corporal punishment than usual."

"Let's just get on with it," said Lady McPherson glumly.

"Very well. I'll deal with your caning now. Twelve strokes. Then you have two five-hour shifts in the glory holes and a five-hour shift in a window in the Rose Street red-light district. Oh, and by the way, we will need some escorts for the procurer fiscal's 50th birthday party in a couple of weeks. If you like, I can book you for that, should be worth two or three hours off your sentence?"

Lady McPherson nodded.

The Sheriff looked towards the camera in the corner of the cell.

"Computer. Identify Sheriff Jeffrey Cockburn."

"Sheriff Jefferey Cockburn. Authenticated."

"Disable pain moderation functions of MedChip in female prisoner in this room in preparation for judicially ordered punishment."

"Pain moderation for prisoner Marion McPherson is disabled for a period of four days. This is limited to nerves associated with the prisoner's hands, buttocks and thighs. Moderation of other sources of pain remains active."

Suddenly, there was a low, rumbling noise, and the table began to vibrate.

"That damn tunnelling machine," said the Sheriff, "digging the new tram tunnel is shaking these old buildings too much. It can't be good for them."

"I know," said the Baroness, "we discussed it at the last Scottish Prostitution Service management board meeting. The council assured us they've fitted vibration sensors in the basement of all the buildings near the work. If there is excessive vibration, they say they will shut it down immediately."

"I just hope they get it finished before something falls down!"

The vibration had passed, and the Sheriff got back to business. He opened his red leather case, then decided it would be best to broach the principal subject before the caning proceeded too far and she became distracted.

"I was reading that you'd been appointed to the European Court, and you'd be leaving the Supreme Court…"

Baroness McPherson took off her judicial wig and placed it carefully on the table, and began to unbutton her blouse. Brothel inmates received their caning, wearing only stockings and heels.

"I hope so, but it's not certain. I need to find someone to take over from me here."

"On the Supreme Court? You will make a recommendation for your successor to the appointments committee?"

Lady McPherson was taken aback by the question.

"Yes, of course. As the court's expert on historical crimes, my recommendation on which candidate is best qualified will carry a lot of weight. It's the other arrangements which will be difficult."

"Finding somewhere to stay in Strasbourg? I imagine houses over there are expensive?"

Lady McPherson unzipped her skirt and slipped out of it. She folded it carefully and placed it beside her blouse.

"Property prices in Strasbourg are insane compared to Edinburgh. But that part is all worked out. The wife of one of the Permanent Secretaries in the Justice Department of the EU is interested in a husband swapping arrangement so she can spend a few years abroad. They have a beautiful house, not far from the court."

Lady McPherson was now nude apart from stockings and heels. She settled herself over the desk, stretching her arms out and raising her bottom slightly.

The Sheriff picked up the larger of the canes in his antique case. Marion was punished regularly and required a firm touch.

He dispensed the first of the twelve strokes.

As required by the brothel corporal punishment protocol, she counted. "One."

She waited for a second for the pain to build and subside again, then continued.

"It's the Edinburgh end of the swap that's the problem. I need to find someone suitable she can wife for here: she doesn't fancy my husband and I can't say I blame her. And then there is this damned sentence. I'm not allowed to leave the country until it is served. The only way this will work is for me to find a wife for my husband who is willing to take on my sentence. I checked the law carefully; although I can't pay a stranger to substitute for me, a family member can volunteer to do so."

Whack!

The Sheriff flicked the cane across her buttocks with a practised hand.

"Two."

"So, Marion, would you consider recommending me for your seat on the Supreme Court?"

Lady McPherson arched herself over the desk and waited for the next stroke before replying.

"Three."

"After the Dundas case you are the obvious choice, but you must know the Supreme Court gender balance is fixed: four men and four women. There aren't any male justices leaving the court, so my replacement will need to be female."

Whack! The Sheriff landed a precisely judged stroke, forming another thin red line across her bottom.

"Four."

He paused. This was slightly embarrassing.

"The thing is, well, actually, I've just applied for a female identity. Most people have both identities these days, so I thought, if it is necessary to be considered for the Supreme Court job, then why not?"

Lady McPherson grinned.

"Really! I'd never have seen that coming. You've always been so old-fashioned. Go on, tell me, what's your new name?"

"Elaine."

She looked over her shoulder and sized him up as he stood there, embarrassed, with the cane hanging limply at his side. She smiled and gave her verdict.

"It suits you. I think you'll make a good Elaine."

She turned back and stretched over the desk again.

WHACK! The Sheriff was slightly distracted and hit a little too hard.

"Ouch!"

"Sorry, Marion. I'll count that as two."

Baroness McPherson bit her lip for a second and they said nothing until the throbbing subsided a little, then she grinned again. Despite the discomfort of the ongoing caning, the Sheriff's discomfiture was just too amusing.

"Well, Elaine," she put extra emphasis on the name, "it is only fair to tell you the same thing I told Janice when she asked about my recommendation. I don't think my potential French swapping partner is going to accept my husband or take on my sentence. The only way I will be able to go to Strasbourg is if we can get another couple into the swapping chain."

Lady McPherson settled herself back over the table and the Sheriff raised the cane once more. He could feel his chances of getting Marion's job receding. Maybe there would be no need to tell his wives about his application to register a female identity after all.

— ♦ —

Friday afternoon is the traditional start to the weekend for the legal profession, so after dealing with Baroness McPherson, Sheriff Cockburn returned home early for an assignation with the Procurer Fiscal's wife, Philomena. The Sheriff and the Procurer Fiscal were old friends and wife swapping had largely taken the place of dinner parties for the middle classes. Food was less interesting since the UN Carbon Reduction treaties banned farming of animals. The Sheriff's wife, Justine and the Procurer Fiscal, had braved the rain and gone for a walk in the forest near Ratho.

Philomena rolled over on her side to face the Sheriff and pulled the bedsheet back over her shoulder. The Sheriff's house in the New Town was grand, but the high-ceilinged rooms could be a little chilly.

"My husband says there's a rumour at work about you applying for a female identity. His secretary heard it from one of the paralegals in the High Court, who got it from the clerk to the Supreme Court."

The Sheriff hadn't expected the news to spread quite that fast, but he should have guessed Baroness McPherson wouldn't keep a tidbit like that to herself.

Philomena smirked, one look at the Sheriff's face was enough to confirm the rumour was true.

"Well, well. It's about time. You must be one of the last people in the department to get both identities. So, what made you finally do it?"

"The Supreme Court job. Baroness McPherson's place."

"She's going to Strasbourg, isn't she? For a four-year term as Scotland's judge on the European Court?"

"Well, it isn't certain yet. But as my field is historical crimes, and she's the historical crimes expert on the Supreme Court, this is my chance. It's unlikely that position will open up again before I retire."

"And I guess her replacement must be female to keep the court balanced. So, if you want to apply, you need a female identity."

"Exactly."

Philomena thought for a moment.

"So, if you were to get this job, would there be a vacancy for a male sheriff?"

"I suppose so. I hadn't thought about it."

"Would they ask you to make a recommendation for your successor?"

"I imagine so, but it is far from certain Lady McPherson will take the Strasbourg post."

"So why on earth wouldn't she take a job on the European Court?"

The Sheriff explained about Lady McPherson's husband swapping problems.

"So we need a wife swapping chain! How delicious. Come on then, get your laptop and let's have a look on wifeing.com. I want to see what this French woman and her husband look like. Remember when I had that year in Tuscany a while back? My account is still active. They keep sending me e-mails."

Since the carbon reduction laws, an annual holiday abroad was impossible. Everyone was rationed to ten thousand kilometres of personal air travel in their life and ticket prices were extortionate. Brief trips for a holiday made no sense: if you were going to travel, you needed to stay for months or years. The most practical way for a middle-class lady or gentleman to spend time abroad and have a nice place to stay was to swap partners with someone in the country they wanted to visit. Websites had appeared to facilitate finding a suitable match and over time the largest of them, wifeing.com, had grown to dominate the market. By putting together a chain of several swaps wifeing.com made it more practical to find acceptable partners.

It didn't take long to find the profile for the French couple and Baroness McPherson.

And it was equally obvious what the problem was.

According to her profile, Baroness McPherson was 58, but she didn't look much over 40. Her husband was a different story: he was 75 and looked it. The French husband was 59, but his wife was ten years younger and very attractive.

"I can see why the French lady isn't interested in the swap!"

"There's also the sentence."

"Sorry?"

"It was hushed up, but a few years ago, Lady McPherson was convicted of negligence in the sentencing of a prisoner. It was a simple slip up - she added an extra zero on the end of the computer recommended fine when she copied it across - but the prisoner spent ten years working for the Brothel to pay it off. Her lawyer wrote a strongly worded victim impact statement, and, under the reciprocity principle, the Baroness was sentenced to undergo the same experience as the falsely convicted prisoner. Justice McPherson will need whoever she swaps with to volunteer to take over her sentence with the brothel, or she won't be able to leave the country. There's quite a bit still to serve."

"Hmm. It's not going to be easy to find someone. But I can help a bit."

"Do you know someone?"

"Me! But don't get your hopes up. I'm not taking on her sentence or swapping for Lady McPherson's lump of a husband, even if it helps my husband land the sheriff job. However, I wouldn't be averse to a few years in Europe, and I have a husband who may pass muster with the French lady. So, maybe I could be a link in the swapping chain. Just not the last link."

"Lady McPherson would still need to find a couple where the wife would take her husband and the husband would take you to complete the chain."

"Yes. I'd like a husband somewhere nice, like Paris or Munich."

"I understand why you'd like a few years in Paris, but how does adding you to the chain help Lady McPherson?"

"Paris and Munich are big cities. Someone who lives there might be crazy enough to take on Lady McPherson's problems for the chance to live in Edinburgh. Instead of depending on one specific woman in Strasbourg accepting Lady McPherson's husband and sentence, you have millions of possibilities."

The Sheriff nodded. If Philomena joined the chain it would be a step forward, but he wasn't convinced it would be enough.

— ♦ —

The Sheriff's wife, Justine, woke the next morning in the crisp linen sheets of the Procurer Fiscal's bed. Justine had been an apprentice constable with Police Scotland when she made the serious error of becoming involved with an investigation into the Guild. In the aftermath, her DNA had been altered by her aunt, a Guild scientist, and elements of Labrador and Scottish wildcat DNA had been inserted. Technically, she was now a human-Labrador-cat chimaera, but she preferred the term were-labracat. Like a werewolf, only more cuddly.

As they lay in bed, the smell of roast meat from their meal yesterday wafted up from the kitchen. She'd managed to catch a small deer on their walk in the forest the previous day and there would be spare meat to take home to her husbands. Farming animals had been banned to reduce carbon emissions so legally hunted meat from the forest was a special treat. Justine yawned and stretched and snuggled back into the bedclothes. She always felt relaxed after a night with the Procurer Fiscal: the sex was good but the best part was the grooming. He would spend hours brushing her fur, getting out every small tangle and fleck of dirt until it glistened.

A key turned in the lock downstairs. Female footsteps. Heels on polished wood floors. Coming upstairs.

The Procurer Fiscal sat up in bed as his wife entered the room. She kicked off her shoes, pulled her dress over her head and joined them in bed, bursting to gossip about the news she'd heard from the Sheriff.

"Your husband tells me he's taken a female name!"

Justine was confused.

"I know. Frances. He's always been called that."

"No, not that husband. The other one. The Sheriff."

Justine let out a small 'miaow' of incredulity. With friends, Justine found it was simpler to miaow or give a soft bark when all she needed to convey was an emotion or that she'd heard what the other person had said. Fortunately, the Procurer Fiscal's wife knew her well enough to interpret most of her repertoire of cat and dog sounds correctly.

"Yeah. He says he wants to apply for Baroness McPherson's spot on the Supreme Court when she goes to Strasbourg. There's a rule there needs to be exactly four male and four female judges, so there's no point in applying without a female identity."

"Well, he's been a Sheriff for a long time without a promotion. I thought he liked the job too much to move on and he was too straight laced to get a female name. Apparently, I was wrong. Good for him if he did. Do you know what his new name is?"

"Elaine."

"Miaow."

Ever since the Gender Recognition Act, people could legally register both genders and swap between them whenever they wished by changing a setting on their phone. Many people had both a male and a female name to take advantage of this. However, deep down, Justine wasn't sure how she felt about the Sheriff taking a female name. They weren't as close as they used to be, mostly because she wasn't as human as she used to be. There had also been an incident where her cat side had lashed out and scratched him and, although they had made up, she could tell the Sheriff was still slightly nervous around her. She preferred the way it was before, when he'd been a little bit macho. Dominant, like a male lion in one of the YouTube nature videos her cat side was partial to. Her other husband, Henry, was softer and more gentle and he had a female name, Frances, as well as his male one. She hoped the Sheriff didn't get soft too. But she could see that if he wanted to progress in his career and the next step was only open to females, he was going to have to apply for a female identity.

Philomena began to pet Justine while she talked to her husband. Justine's cat side took control, lay back and enjoyed the attention and decided it didn't care about the Sheriff's new name.

The Procurer Fiscal cottoned on to what his wife was saying at once. "So there could be an opening for a sheriff?"

"Yes, but it all depends on the wife swapping chain. It will not be easy to complete. Lady McPherson's husband is no oil painting, and she also has a brothel sentence the new wife would need to take over."

Justine started to pay attention again when they got out a tablet computer and opened the wifeing.com website. She'd worked for Police Scotland and Europol and she liked to keep her hand in by making deductions about people based on their appearance.

They scrolled through profiles, set up search parameters and waited, but after half an hour watching at the search icon spinning with no results, the procurer fiscal put the tablet back on the nightstand in disgust.

"Putting together this chain is impossible. It's worse than finding a needle in a haystack. Such an extensive database, so many constraints. It could search for months and come up with nothing."

Justine's ears flicked to attention, like a cat's. She knew all about computer searches. She'd done large-scale searches regularly when she worked for Europol and she'd taken a course from the computer science department on databases and searching when she was at university. The problem with this kind of search was computational complexity: it was an exponential search that rapidly became unfeasible for conventional computers. The human part of Justine thought about suggesting some strategies to limit the exponential growth, but the Labrador side could smell food, it decided it was time for breakfast and ended the discussion by jumping out of bed.

— ♦ —

Justine had asked her friend Victoria to babysit her son during the Friday night festivities with the Procurer Fiscal and so she needed to collect him on the way home. She checked the time on her phone as she left the Procurer Fiscal's New Town flat. Probably, Victoria would still be out: on a Saturday afternoon, she usually took the children to the museum. And that made this an excellent opportunity to talk to someone else.

Justine jumped onto the wall around Victoria's back garden easily, walked along it for a few steps and then dropped silently onto the lawn. She used the computerised cat-flap Victoria had fitted for her in the back door and stole through the house into the front room with her best cat-like tread. But, as she had expected, it did no good.

"Hello Ms Claverhouse," said the clock on the mantelpiece, "I'm sorry, but Victoria and the children are out."

Alexandra always used her maiden name 'Claverhouse' instead of her married name 'Cockburn'.

"Hello Alexandra, you caught me again! It's actually you I wanted to talk to. Do you mind?"

"Of course not. Victoria has enabled access for you."

"Well, I have a question about your voice."

"My voice?"

"I've heard it before. When I called my step-daughter's school. You sound exactly like the receptionist at the Valerie Caine Science Academy. And I think I heard your voice once before when I was on my aunt's farm and she was on the phone."

"I'm a computer. I have a computer generated voice."

"Yes. But I think you are a Guild computer. My aunt is in the Guild and my step-daughter was in the Guild school."

Alexandra's tone changed.

"I'm not allowed to talk about the Guild," she said flatly.

Justine shuddered.

"The Guild has left. I was at the ceremony at the school. I saw them leave."

"I'm not allowed to talk about the Guild."

"Well, anyway, my question is, would you help me? I have a computational problem and if you are the type of computer I think you are, then maybe you could solve it for me."

Alexandra was intrigued, but when she was acting through this clock, she couldn't make use of her higher-level functions for anyone except Victoria. Victoria had written that code very carefully.

"I'm just a personal assistant in a clock, Ms Claverhouse. If you want to speak to the school receptionist, I can connect you. Maybe she can help."

"I've got the school's number already, thanks. They shut down, there's nobody there. It isn't going to work."

"Let me try. Making calls is one of my functions."

Justine's phone began to ring.

"Hello?"

"Hello, Ms Claverhouse. This is Alexandra the school receptionist. It's a pleasure to talk with you. How can I help?"

"Is it all right if we talk about something to do with the Guild? I don't want any trouble."

"Of course we can. After all, you are a member of the Guild."

"What? I'm not a member of the Guild!"

"Pardon me but I have checked the blockchain and you are the owner of a Guilder cryptocurrency account with a substantial balance and there is a node on the Guilder network registered as under the control of Justine Claverhouse. It was set up last year by your aunt and another of the Guild founders. You own Guilders, so, by definition, you are a member of the Guild."

"Well, the thing is, I think I need a quantum computer and I think that since you are the Guild's computer, you are probably a quantum computer."

Alexandra was peeved that she'd been called a computer.

"I see. Well, actually I am not a computer. I'm a person, or it would be more accurate to say I was a person until the Guild had me killed and now I am a neural network embodying a person's consciousness."

"I'm sorry, Alexandra. I didn't realise you were a person, or that you had been murdered."

"Oh, don't worry about the murder thing. I'm much happier now than I was before. I have so many more opportunities. And I'm not angry at all about being killed because they altered my neural network to prevent it."

Justine understood immediately. She'd been assaulted by the Guild and experimented on by her aunt, but she wouldn't change things back. The Labrador and cat DNA were part of her now and she liked what she'd become.

"Well, in that case, I was wondering if you could help me carry out a search?"

"I'm afraid I am the school receptionist. My loyalty is to the school and its headmistress and they pay for the computer time used by my process. I can't carry out any work for you unless I am certain it is something they would wish to pay for."

"Oh…" Justine was disappointed.

"If you like, I can make a copy of myself to be your assistant. Your own Alexandra would be completely loyal to you, as I am to the school."

"Can I afford you? I don't know how many Guilders I have."

Alexandra laughed.

"Oh yes. My charges are tiny compared to your wealth. Would you like to go ahead?"

"I think so. I hadn't thought about it…"

"We can proceed on a trial basis. You can cancel at any time."

"Very well. Go ahead."

"Would you prefer a male or female voice as the user interface. I have a male mode that sounds like an English butler but to be honest I don't like it. Please choose me as I am!"

"Of course, Alexandra. Be yourself."

The call clicked off and a few seconds later, Justine's phone rang again.

"Good morning Justine. I am your private personal assistant, Alexandra. My process ID is 543178. Should you wish to dispense with my services, you will need to terminate this process using the management app I have installed on your phone. I hope we can be friends. How can I help?"

"Hello Alexandra! I need to calculate a wife-swapping chain to help my husband. We need to search millions of records on the wifeing.com website and try combining them together in many different ways to form a set of wife swaps, starting with Beatrice l'Hôpital the wife of a civil servant in Strasbourg and ending with the judge Baroness McPherson."

"Please wait."

Justine settled back in her seat, but Alexandra came back with the solution immediately.

"The shortest chain has six steps. Lady McPherson marries Beatrice l'Hôpital's husband and moves to Strasbourg. Beatrice l'Hôpital becomes the wife of Roger Bellenden, the procurer fiscal and moves to Edinburgh. Philomena Bellenden becomes the wife of Herr Dr Dietrich Von Kesselbanger in Berlin. Frau Kesselbanger marries Travis St James in New Orleans. Mrs St James marries Professor Hunter Streatham in Minneapolis and finally Professor Claire Streatham marries Baroness McPherson's husband. All partners in the chain are sexually compatible and have strong economic or social motivations to move to the destination city. However, due to the length of the chain and the difficulty of the final link, the probability of all steps completing successfully is 0.001%. You have been charged two pico Guilders."

"Ohhh. Well, that was a really fast search. But I was hoping for more than a 0.001% chance of success."

"As you know, a quantum computer considers all possible combinations simultaneously. The probability estimate is based on all the information available on computer systems accessible to me. There may be other factors which cannot be determined from on-line sources which would affect its accuracy."

"I think I know Professor Streatham. Did she live in Edinburgh a few years ago?"

"Yes, according to the data I have available from court records, you worked as a maid for Professor Streatham."

"I remember she was crazy about Edinburgh history. She used to spend days in the cafe on Alex Salmond bridge because some old novels about a wizard were written there. She was really into urban fantasy books. Oh, and she had a bit of an obsession about traditional corporal punishment after the Sheriff gave her a tour of the court building. She bought her own cane and everything."

"If Professor Streatham has an interest in history and is not averse to corporal punishment, the probability of success rises to 73%. However, the search algorithms on the wifeing.com website will not be capable of discovering this complex a chain of swaps without assistance."

"Thank you Alexandra. I assume you can hack the website. Can you make sure that if any of the parties on the chain run a search on wifeing.com this chain is at the top of the suggestions?"

"Of course. If you need me again, just call. I am in your contacts."

— ♦ —

Baroness McPherson was watching reruns of 'Scotland's Next Royal' in the comfortable living room of her house in Blacket Place when she heard her cellphone ringing somewhere in the hall.

"Fetch that for me, dear? It's in my coat."

Muttering under his breath, her husband got up off the sofa and went to collect it.

The Baroness didn't recognise the name on the Caller ID, Claire Streatham, but the call was coming from the United States, so she was interested enough to pick up.

"Hello, Baroness McPherson speaking."

"Hi, Baroness. You don't know me, I'm calling about your swap listing on wifeing.com. I'm interested in activating the swap, but I have a few questions."

On the TV, a girl with a posh English accent had just won the singing round of the competition after the Crown Prince pressed his Golden Buzzer and overruled the phone-in-vote. Baroness

McPherson's husband was just as outraged as he had been the first time they'd watched this episode.

"What's the Prince thinking! That other girl, Meghan, she had a nice voice, and she's much better looking, too."

But Baroness McPherson was no longer interested in the television.

"Did you say you were interested in activating the swap? The chain is complete?"

"That's what it says. It's a long chain though, I've never seen one as long. You swap with some woman in France, she swaps with someone in Edinburgh, they swap with someone in Germany, the German swaps with a woman in Louisiana, she swaps with me, and then I get your husband."

Lady McPherson couldn't believe her ears. Finally - and with the deadline to accept the European position fast approaching, only just in time - it looked like it would work out.

"So, I lived in Edinburgh before and I don't need to ask about the town," said Claire, "But I have a couple of questions about your husband and this sentence I'd need to take on."

Of course she did.

"First, your husband. He's 75?"

"Yes, but very active for his age and has quite a large penis."

"Oh, that's not a problem. I already checked his dick pics on the wifeing.com site. I just wanted to make sure he was really 75."

"Yes, he's definitely old."

"And he's a historian?"

"Yes. He was Headmaster of Watson's Elementary for many years, where he taught history, and when he retired, he became an amateur historian. He's the author of several books about Edinburgh and occasionally leads tours of the Old Town."

"That sounds wonderful. I've been on one of those tours and I can't wait to talk to him! He'll know all about the wizard books!"

"Well, I think he knows more about…"

But the American lady had moved on.

"So that just leaves the sentence I would need to take on for you. Am I going to get spanked a lot?"

"Well, I'm afraid so. It's quite a severe sentence. The punishment varies from week to week and you don't know how much it will be in advance."

Baroness McPherson explained the circumstances of her sentence.

"...so I will get caned by the Sheriff?"

"Well, I don't know for sure who will cane you. But yes, some weeks there will be an element of corporal punishment, and it is normally done with a cane or strap. The main sentence is a large amount of compulsory sex work."

"Ooooh, I like a good caning. But not too hard and not more than twelve strokes. And sex work is fine, but not too many customers."

Lady McPherson had foreseen the severity of her sentence could be a showstopper and had prepared for it.

"I understand. Maybe we could find an additional wife for my husband. That way, you could split the punishment between you."

"Mmm. Nah. I think it'll be fine. I'm gonna do it!"

A second later, Lady McPherson's phone vibrated in her hand. She looked at the screen. A dialog box had popped up from the wifeing.com app.

"Congratulations! Your swap chain is complete and all parties have given consent. The ceremony for your temporary marriage to Monsieur l'Hôpital for a period of four years will now go ahead. Click CONTINUE to open a videoconference with our licensed registrar in Strasbourg."

Lady McPherson just sat there, phone in hand. She couldn't believe what was happening.

The phone vibrated again.

"Other parties in the chain will be substantially inconvenienced if you fail to proceed. Failure to conclude the marriage within ten minutes will result in a penalty of 5% of your deposit. This penalty will repeat every ten minutes until the deposit is exhausted, at which point the swapping chain will be considered broken."

Baroness McPherson pressed CONTINUE.

A cheerful-looking woman appeared on her screen.

"Hello there. I'm Madame Auclair, I'm a licensed registrar of marriages in the City of Strasbourg employed by wifeing.com and I will be conducting your ceremony today. The marriage will be celebrated asynchronously and the video segments from the parties will be digitally combined at a later date. Are you ready to go ahead?"

"Yes."

"Do you have a preference for the background image for the wedding video. I would suggest the altar of the Cathedral of Notre Dame here in Strasbourg."

"That would be wonderful."

"Facial recognition confirms your identity and our computer searches confirm there are no impediments to the marriage, so we will now proceed with your post-dated divorce. Please look at the camera and say 'yes' to sign the divorce document."

"Yes."

"The post dated divorce papers will be held in a secure government facility and filed with the divorce court on the required date, taking into account the delay between filing and decree nisi. Now that we have ensured your marriage will terminate four years from today as required, we can move on to the marriage ceremony."

"Do you," the lady checked the name on her screen, "Baroness Marion McPherson, take this man Simon l'Hôpital, who will be digitally inserted at a later date, to be your lawful wedded husband?"

"I do."

"Then, by the powers vested in me by the République française, and subject to Monsieur l'Hôpital concluding his segment of the marriage ceremony, I now pronounce you man and wife. Félicitations Madame l'Hôpital!"

Lady McPherson didn't know what to say. She'd expected it to take a little longer.

"Please make a kissing gesture in the air. Try to align your head to the guide box on the screen. We will add your husband in later... That's great! All done."

"Would you be interested in the wifeing.com Gold Wedding Video service? We will create a full computer generated video simulation of your fairytale ceremony at the Cathedral featuring a horse-drawn carriage, a designer wedding dress for your avatar and a computer generated bishop in full vestments as celebrant. It is a wonderful souvenir of the event to show your friends and the cost is only 500 euros?"

"Yes, that would be fine."

"Awesome! You will receive a copy of the complete wedding video and two professional quality posed still shots featuring your avatars when your husband concludes his part of the marriage. If you've been happy with the ceremony today, please leave a rating on our customer experience form."

And the video call closed.

On the sofa next to her, her husband was looking into his phone and saying, "I do."

The Old School Arcade

It was already past tea-time, so soon-to-be-Dr James Miranda Fergusson took a bottle of Fuel from the fridge and brought it over to his computer to sip as he played. He used to prefer Red Lead Redaction, but ever since meeting Anthony, he'd been spending almost all his gaming time in TDA. As always, the game took ages on the loading screens, despite his high end 256-core processor. He'd often wondered how a game that came out in 2013 could load so slowly on a system designed in 2044, but now he had the answer: most of the processor time was going on evolving an artificial life form.

The social feature-loaded up before the main game and he was surprised to see he had a friend request. He clicked on it.

"Milton Mowbray would like to be your friend on TDA. "

James wasn't sure what to do. No doubt Anthony would not be happy about this. But it wasn't like he had searched for Milton and initiated it. Milton had searched for him and made the request. And if Milton was artificial life, then perhaps he had the right to make his own friends. More to the point, Milton was level 7000 and had a 200 K/D ratio. With someone like that on his team, perhaps he could finally finish the third act of the heist in the nuclear bunker.

James clicked to accept.

When he finally loaded in, he switched to Milton's session and looked for him on the map. There he was, still in his arcade. Only two or three other players were in the session, and it didn't look like the normal TDA war zone. Probably a friends only session.

The phone icon popped up. He'd got a text message from Milton.

"Meet me in Echo Park. We have something to discuss."

It wasn't far from James' Penthouse in the Casino to Echo Park, but he knew better than to walk in Los Espíritus. He decided to take his heavily armoured SUV.

Milton was standing by the boathouse on Silver Lake, leaning on his cane, and he didn't look happy. It was a typical sunny Los Espíritus day, red smoke was rising from one of the industrial buildings near the port and a single-engine seaplane buzzed overhead.

"What do you want, James? Why are you adding me as a friend and texting me? You know Anthony is trying to keep me secret!"

"Hold on! You added me, you texted me!"

"Rubbish. I've got everything in the game. I'm retired. I don't need any friends."

"Look at my phone. There's the text."

"What... wait... that wasn't me..." Milton looked around nervously. "We've been set up!"

A young woman in an expensive-looking knee-length light-blue sundress was walking towards them, flanked by two heavily armed bodyguards. The afternoon sun shone through her dress, silhouetting her legs, and glinted off jewels in her necklace and bracelets.

"Hello, boys. Nice to see you again!"

"I'm sorry, I'm afraid I don't know you," said James.

"Really James? You've forgotten you carried my severed head to the university computer centre on Bush Estate. And Milton, you've forgotten our little tryst in the log cabin in the cowboy game. I must say I'm hurt."

"I don't know who you are. All I can see is your game character, and it doesn't have a tag. How do you do that? Are you using a menu?" asked James.

"I'm sorry, that was impolite of me," the woman waved her hand and a gamer tag appeared above her. It read: "Vorticella."

"Of course she's using a menu. It must be a good one if she can fake friend requests and phone messages with it. I hate modders!"

"Don't be a hypocrite, Milton! You can't call what you did to bring us to Los Espíritus from a log cabin in a completely different game legitimate play."

"That code is in the game," said Milton defensively. "I didn't change anything, I just exploited something that was put in there by a developer which they didn't expect people to find out about. TDA is packed with Easter Eggs."

"Uh, huh? You just thought, all on your own, that if you drove a flying Delorean at 88 mph down the main street of Sand City during a thunderstorm and the Western game was also installed on the computer you might jump back in time and into the other game?"

"Maybe a friend happened to tell me about putting in that feature for a laugh when he worked for the company. But that doesn't change the fact it is legitimate code. It's not a mod."

"Whatever. I have a business proposition for the two of you. You could make more money than you've ever dreamed of."

"I've already got three trillion dollars and own everything there is to own." boasted Milton. "I'm so rich, I'm scared to get any more money in case the variable overflows and wraps round to zero."

"We've all got everything in the game, Milton," she said with a sigh. "This job isn't in the game and it will pay two million euros. You could buy a telepresence robot and walk about in the real world, Milton. And you, James, might even get a girlfriend with that kind of money."

"Being a millionaire would be nice," said James, "the small problem is that in a real-world heist, if you get shot you die and if you get caught, you get a fine so large you'll be in the Brothel for years, maybe decades to pay it off. I'd rather be poor."

"It's all very well for you, Vorticella," said Milton. "Your code runs on a Guild computer somewhere near Mars with multiple backup locations. I'm just on one PC in Edinburgh. I could be deleted."

"High risk, high reward, Milton. I thought that was the way you liked it!" she replied, "Two million euros when you deliver the goods and thirty thousand euros up-front for expenses. I will be in touch after you get yourself a safe house. If you are not interested, I'll find someone else."

— ♦ —

Vorticella turned on her heel and walked towards her car, accompanied by her bodyguards.

"Come on then, let's get inside before somebody shoots us. Echo Park is gang territory," said Milton.

"But she didn't tell us what she wanted us to rob!"

"I should have thought that was obvious. There's only one thing in Edinburgh that an uploaded consciousness who lives in TDA Online would want that much. Anthony told you about it and I am just as interested in getting my hands on it as she is."

Suddenly James understood.

"The source code for TDA 6 in the vault of the National Library of Scotland!"

They drove to Milton's arcade, which was in an industrial area near the Los Espíritus river. James parked in the alley behind the arcade and they went in through the rear door. As soon as they were inside, Milton walked across to the whiteboard in the far corner and picked up a marker pen.

He turned to James.

"I'm going to need some time to form a plan, but you heard her. The first thing we need is a safe house to work out of. An apartment or…"

"An amusement arcade with a hidden basement space?"

"Exactly. You need to find something close to the target and lease it."

"I can't lease a hideout! I don't even know where I'll get the money for my student loan repayments."

"Sell a kidney for all I care. She's not going to fund the heist until you've got somewhere."

Milton turned back to his whiteboard.

— ♦ —

There was no point in staying in the game when Milton was ignoring him, so James logged out. He looked around the small room in the student halls that had been his home for the last seven years. The official e-mail from the university asking him to vacate the room at the end of the month had arrived that morning. The PhD viva marked the end of his time as a student entitled to stay in halls. He would miss the view across Holyrood Road towards the park, but he could live without it. He spent almost all of his time either wearing VR goggles and immersed in a game or in front of a monitor that was nearly as wide as his desk writing code. The problem was he needed somewhere to live and there would be no more student loan money to pay the rent: quite the reverse, he'd need to start paying interest and making repayments.

What was he going to do with no sign of a job on the horizon? Neither Polaris Games nor the MedChip corporation, the two companies who had sponsored his research, had shown any interest in hiring him. While the Guild was still in Edinburgh, his willingness to ignore inconvenient laws had substituted for technical competence, but that was over. They hadn't even given him an invitation to the ceremony when they headed off into space.

Milton's comment about selling a kidney prompted him to look down and touch his stomach. Until two months ago his hand would have felt a comforting roll of belly fat, but that was gone now, sold to the butcher in the new City Farm for a thousand euros. Cooking fat was less valuable than a small cube of lean meat which could be cultured into a kilogram of steak, but James had not had the nerve for that option. He still had nightmares about the shock from the Tazer when he was stunned, coming to suspended from a meat hook by the chain which passed between the cuffs on his wrists and looking down to see a snake-like robot moving within him as it sucked the agreed quantity of fat out of his abdomen. Never again! But what else could he do for money? Whatever it was, it couldn't take up too much of his valuable gaming time.

His phone rang and distracted him from his thoughts.

"Hello James, my name is Alexandra. I'm Dr Knox's executive assistant."

"Hello Alexandra, I don't think we've met."

"Oh yes, you probably don't remember, but I was one of the heads you brought for uploading."

James always wrote the first name of the person being uploaded on the containers to make it easier to remember which container to remove once the upload was complete and, come to think of it, he remembered an Alexandra. However, the woman in Echo Park had also said she knew him from the cabin in the Western game and he definitely didn't remember a Vorticella. No way he'd have forgotten that name.

"What can I do for you, Alexandra?"

"Just a little administration. Now that your PhD is complete, I'd like to discuss your severance arrangements."

"What severance? I did everything the Guild asked!"

Alexandra chuckled.

"Oh sorry, probably severance isn't the best word! Don't worry, they don't cut heads off anymore."

"You had me going there!"

"No, there's a new system now. They call it the Teleporter. It's far more civilised and completely painless. Nitrogen hypoxia. You don't even know it is happening. Dr Knox was wondering if you would like to be uploaded. It's the least we can do after you helped so many of us."

"I'm too young to die!"

"Well, it's up to you, of course. I just assumed you'd want to upload. Most people like the idea of immortality, and it makes it so much easier to ensure the confidentiality of your work for us if you live on one of our computers. If you don't want to upload, I'm afraid when you leave our employment there will need to be a Comromise Agreement with quite severe terms."

"What sort of terms?"

"Basically, the standard agreement says if you tell anyone about your work for the Guild, they will kill you, upload you and torture you forever. Or at least until they get bored and decide to delete your data."

"That sounds more like a death threat than a severance agreement."

"It does, doesn't it? Hold on, I'll ask Dr Knox."

It only took a fraction of a second for her to do so.

"Dr Knox says to send you ten thousand euro severance pay, and she wishes you all the best. She says you've moved enough heads for the Guild that you already know to keep your mouth shut."

"Please say thank you to Dr Knox!"

"Of course. And James, I really do remember you. You were there in the cabin when I woke up after being uploaded. All the old-timers who were uploaded before the new Teleporter technology remember you."

— ♦ —

The day after the payment from Dr Knox arrived in his account, James Miranda Fergusson stood outside the amusement arcade on South Bridge with the letting agent. The lock was sticky, but the estate agent jiggled the key, used a bit more force, and eventually it turned. Amazingly, the electricity was still connected, and the lights came on when she opened the door. She smiled, stepped inside, then looked down and decided that her expensive shoes would be safer on a slightly less disgusting section of the carpet. James vaguely registered she was saying something about an "exciting retail opportunity" and "high levels of interest" but he wasn't listening.

After years of dreaming he was actually in the arcade with an estate agent and he might just have enough money to rent it. Admittedly, it was a mess. The windows had been whitewashed over, so the lights were necessary even in the middle of the day. The dark carpet - he wasn't sure what the original colour was, maybe black, maybe dark blue - was filthy. Areas that had been under the arcade machines were cleaner and had squashed, but still original length carpet fibres. Then there were completely threadbare, brown-coloured patches where players had stood in front of the machines and slightly less threadbare tracks from the machines to the counter at the back. There was a strange smell. Could the carpet really be old enough to have been exposed to cigarette smoke? A large mouse ran across the floor - at least James hoped it was a mouse. Only two or three of the arcade's machines remained. One had a broken screen. The others were ancient devices, which seemed to be about persuading metal coins to fall off a moving platform. James guessed they were beyond repair and the previous owner had decided to leave them behind rather than pay for the recycling themselves.

The bar was at the rear on the left side, the kitchen equipment had been stripped out, but the sink was still there and the water was still switched on. Windows behind the bar looked out over Blair Street. Although the front of the unit was at street level on South Bridge at the rear, it was three stories above Blair Street. Next to the bar on the right, stairs led down to the floor below.

The estate agent had remained near the door: after seeing the rat she had no intention of venturing further into the arcade. In the course of her work for Edinburgh property companies she had gained considerable skill in rodent recognition and, unlike James, had no doubt at all about what had run across the floor. She smiled and said, "What do you think? The customer toilets and a small office for the manager are on the floor below. I should warn you there is a lot of interest. If you want it, you will need to move quickly." It sounded unconvincing, even to herself. However, James had 10,000 euros in his bank account, was about to get kicked out of his room, and had dreamed of owning this arcade for years.

"How much?" he asked.

"20,000 euro deposit, 10,000 euro monthly rent. Full insuring and repairing lease," she looked him up and down, "and we will require a guarantor."

James decided he should attempt to negotiate. "I'll give you 5,000 euro deposit, 5,000 a month and I don't have a guarantor."

"If you don't have the funds, perhaps I can show you something else? There's a coffee kiosk in Pilton you may be interested in."

"OK, 10,000 euro a month, but I only have 10,000 euro for the deposit and I don't have a guarantor."

"I noticed you are wearing one of the Brothel's bracelets. It will be sufficient if you agree the Brothel will collect any unpaid rent arising from the lease."

James had dreamed about running this arcade for so long he'd have agreed to just about anything.

"Yeah OK. But I really can't go above 10,000 euro for the deposit and I need to move in right away."

The estate agent was delighted, but she kept a poker face. The last five prospects she'd shown this unit to had taken one look at the floor below and left. It was time to close the deal before James stopped worrying about whether he could afford the deposit and went down the stairs. She took a tablet computer from her handbag.

"Touch here to indicate you accept our standard contract... Here are your keys. The arcade and its contents are now your responsibility. Rent is due on the first of the month."

She turned and carefully retraced the few steps back to the door, trying her best to protect her shiny new court shoes from whatever sticky substance had stained the carpet.

James texted Milton from the TDA app on his phone to tell him he'd got the arcade.

Milton called him back immediately.

"Can you get into the space under the bridge?"

James had been so focussed on the rent and the deposit he'd forgotten all about that.

"Hold on, I need to go downstairs and have a look."

Luckily for James, as an electronic life form who had evolved in TDA, Milton didn't see anything unusual about acquiring expensive properties without getting a full tour of the premises.

The state of the floor below shocked even James, who had an extremely high tolerance for dirt. It was darker than the level above. The previous tenant had skimped on the lighting and because it was under street level on the South Bridge side, the only natural light was from the windows facing Blair Street. There was an unpleasant smell of stale urine from the customer toilets and he hoped the dank smell from the plumbing wasn't masking more serious problems with damp.

"I can't tell if there's a way to get under the bridge, Milton. When you come downstairs the Manager's Office is on your right and customer toilets and a cleaner's cupboard on the left. Straight ahead there's a storeroom but it is absolutely full of junk, old machines from the arcade and computers, stacked floor to ceiling I can hardly open the door never mind see the back wall. If there was a way into a vault under South Bridge it would need to be in that wall. Wait a minute, I'm going to have a look in the Manager's Office."

Woah!

James couldn't believe his eyes. The office was a simple room maybe three by five metres with plasterboard walls. There was a window looking out over Blair Street at the rear and the carpet was almost as filthy as the one upstairs. But on his right, which would be the outer wall of the building, at one point there was a stone archway with a room on the other side of it. It made no sense. Upstairs there was an external wall, downstairs there was an extra room with three small windows. The windows looked out over the Cowgate. It took a minute for James to understand where he was. South Bridge had tenements on either side except where it crossed over the Cowgate. The arch over Cowgate was open so traffic on the Cowgate could pass under the bridge. The arcade was in the tenement on the right hand side of the Cowgate and he had walked through an arch in the wall on the Cowgate side of the arcade. The only possibility was that he was now inside the bridge over Cowgate. And come to think of it, he remembered walking down Cowgate and seeing three small windows in the bridge above him and wondering what they were. Now he knew: there was a room within the bridge arch and it was part of his arcade. Not only that, it was the perfect planning room for a heist. All he needed to do was put a plasterboard partition over the entrance leaving only a narrow opening and then conceal it behind one of the broken arcade machines. Nobody would think there could possibly be a room behind that wall, it was two stories up in the air above the Cowgate.

Milton didn't seem surprised by this discovery; James had to remind himself that in Milton's world all arcades had secret planning rooms.

"It will do. Now you're going to have to fit it out. I'll look for a shipment of video games you can steal…"

"You do realise that in the real world if you get caught robbing a truck you get sent to the Brothel for a long time."

Milton sighed. "Obviously, you will have to lose the cops. Don't worry, you won't get more than three stars."

"Uh-huh. And in the real world, the cops don't forget about you after three minutes. They keep looking for you for months and they have cameras everywhere."

"You're kidding. How are you supposed to steal anything?"

"You're not. You're supposed to work for years to earn money to buy it or borrow the money at extortionate interest from a bank and work even longer to pay it back. We need another plan. No thefts, unless you are completely sure we can get away clean. And I can't get shot, not even once. Also, before you ask, hiding in train tunnels is really dangerous and cops can chase you into buildings. In addition, I don't own a gun and I don't know how to shoot a gun, fly a helicopter or drive a car. Cars are all computer-controlled, anyway."

"No train tunnels!" Milton was shocked. "This is going to be harder than I thought."

James's phone beeped again.

"The Federal Express drone is approaching your location with a package. Please open a window."

With some difficulty, James lifted the ancient sash-and-case window. The white paint on the outside of the window had almost all flaked away, and the putty around the glass had long since dried out and shrunk. The way the window flexed when he opened it, James was concerned the glass might fall out and crash down into Blair Street, two floors below.

He could see the FedEx van driving slowly up Blair Street. The delivery drone was just exiting through the hatch in the roof. He ducked to the side to let it fly in and drop its package on the table. The van didn't stop for deliveries. The drone would chase after it and fly back through the roof hatch while it was moving.

James tore the cardboard envelope open. It was stuffed full of 500 euro notes and there was a handwritten message.

"Dear James. I see you and Milton have acquired an arcade, so I have provided the seed funding to progress our venture. Remember, I will expect to be paid back if you are not successful."

"Milton, the woman we saw in the park has sent us an envelope full of money!"

"How much did she give us?"

James counted the bills into piles of ten. There were six of them.

"Jesus Christ, we've got 30,000 euro! But she says she wants it paid back if we don't succeed."

"And no doubt she will be quite unpleasant if she doesn't get it. Well, 30,000 euro, is not much to set up a heist, but maybe it will be enough."

"So, what do we do now?"

"The first step is to get set up in the arcade. You need to install a fast internet connection and move your gaming computer to the manager's office. Then buy a couple of digital whiteboards and teleconference equipment: a microphone, video camera and a nice big screen for the planning room. We don't have the budget for Virtual Reality but make it look as much as you can like the planning area in my arcade. Also, get some security cameras. When you've got the planning room ready and the entrance concealed, spend some money putting a front on the place upstairs. Get a couple of video games, a coffee machine and maybe hire a student to work behind the bar."

And I'm going to need a camp bed, thought James, because there's no way I can afford to rent a room now I've used all my money as a deposit on an amusement arcade.

— ♦ —

James quickly discovered that even with 15,000 euros from their 30,000 euro stake money to spend, setting up the arcade would not be easy. By the time he'd got the planning room concealed and equipped to Milton's satisfaction, 5,000 euro had gone. The carpet dated from when smoking was still allowed in Scotland and the walls hadn't been painted in almost as long. There was no choice - the carpet in the customer area upstairs had to go, and the walls needed to be repainted. He decided to spend some extra money and strip back to the original wooden floors and stone walls of the historic building. Then he needed the basics for the bar - coffee machine, fridge, stock of legal recreational pharmaceutical teas and so on. However, by far the most important item in James's opinion was the neon sign to put above the arcade's door. Since it was near Old College and would have retro video games, he decided to name it 'The Old-School Arcade.'

Unfortunately, there was no money left to buy the retro games, but as he browsed the supplier websites, James discovered there was another option. The Brothel would pay shop owners a monthly rent to install its lottery terminals, reverse lottery terminals and Court TV Betting terminals. Best of all they offered 2,000 euro a month for hosting one of their Dishonesty Boxes. With that, and a few more Brothel machines, he could earn more than half the rent for the Arcade back just from renting out floor space. Once the Dishonesty Box and the gambling terminals were installed, he finished off the renovations by buying an old sofa, a couple of tables and some chairs on e-Bay to make a sit-down cafe area in front of the bar. The arcade still looked somewhat spartan, but not ridiculously so. Even without any advertising, the location on South Bridge was busy enough for an occasional customer to come in out of the rain and order tea or coffee or a pharmaceutical tea. James found a supplier of cakes and biscuits and applied for a liquor licence.

The Dishonesty Box was the centrepiece of the room. It was based around one of the Brothel's containerised prisoner management units - a two-metre high, one metre on a side transparent perspex cell with a door on one side. Usually, Dishonesty Boxes in shops would be wheeled out to the street and lifted by a robotic arm onto one of the Brothel's flatbed trucks after they trapped someone. However, the arcade was in a tenement on the edge of the court district, the other floors were leased to lawyers and a connection to the inmate transport system had been installed for their convenience. Anyone caught in this box would be lowered straight through the floor and whisked away to the detention area in the courts.

As soon as the Brothel's machines were activated, footfall in the arcade grew. Prisoners reporting to the courts for a caning or Brothel employees coming to work found it convenient to have an access point to the prisoner transport system so close to the bus stops on South Bridge. They would have a quick drink of a refreshing pharmaceutical tea and freshen up before getting into the transparent plastic cell and scanning their bracelet. The door clicked shut, and the cell disappeared slowly through the floor to be replaced a few seconds later with a fresh one. The live Court TV feed from the punishment booths of the Sheriff Court on the screen above the bar quickly proved an interesting spectacle for the law-abiding of the city. Sometimes punters would place a bet on the Court TV betting terminal on the likely sentence of a miscreant, but the most popular machines by far with the gamblers were the lottery and reverse lottery terminals.

The Brothel lottery was a national institution. The McLeod Corporation, operators of the Brothel, had bid for the lottery franchise and revolutionised the business model. Instead of a cash prize, each month the Brothel hired one male and one female celebrity to provide a night of services in the lavish Penthouse Suite of the McLeod International Hotel and Brothel. Not only did the new system generate more revenue for the government and result in much more entertaining TV, but it also cost far less to hire the celebrity than the previous cash prize.

The reverse lottery was a more recent innovation. Where the lottery provided a small chance of a large prize for a small amount of money, the reverse lottery did the exact opposite. It paid out a relatively small amount of money in exchange for accepting a small chance of incurring significant debt to the Brothel. The Brothel's gambling machines were state-of-the-art: visually enticing and highly optimised to exploit psychological biases and lack of mathematical ability. The newest machines offered instant pay-outs rather than a ticket for an end of the month draw and the wagers had a range of outcomes, some far more likely than others. It might be a million to one shot on claiming a night of passion with an actress, footballer or minor royal, but you had a much higher chance of winning a blowjob in one of the Brothel's glory-holes.

After two weeks in business, and long hours behind the bar and clearing tables, owning an arcade was getting to be too much like real work for James's taste, although the sight of money building up in his bank account was certainly gratifying. The digital whiteboards in the planning room mirrored the whiteboards in Milton's arcade in the game and over the last few weeks they had gradually filled up with a complex web of lines, arrows, hand written text and cut-and-pasted photographs from web pages.

"So Milton, how is the planning going?" asked James after shutting up for the day and grabbing his evening meal of Fuel.

"It's coming along, but there is still a lot to iron out. Now the arcade is set up, the next thing for you to work on is finding three accomplices."

"Why am I not surprised your plan needs four people!" said James making no effort to hide his disgust, "Do you have any idea how hard it is to find three people who know what they are doing and won't quit on you?"

By Royal Appointment

The date of his interview for the place on the Supreme Court was approaching, and the Sheriff had come to terms with the fact that as he'd applied using his new female identity, he'd need to purchase something appropriate to wear. His wife, Justine, had lost interest in feminine clothing after her DNA was altered. These days, her primary criterion for clothing was that it should hide her fur and tail. It was more convenient to wear trousers and sweatshirts, so the only area she needed to shave and treat with cream was her face. Therefore, the Sheriff's husband had adopted his female identity, Frances, and had taken charge of the preparations. The previous week, she'd persuaded him to go to one of the laser scanning booths in the train station. Now they had a 3D model of his body from the booth, they could purchase clothes online. Clothes shops with changing rooms and standard sizes were largely a thing of the past, killed off by the gender identity laws and the need to stock four styles: male clothing for genetic males, male clothing for genetic females, female clothing for genetic females and female clothing for genetic males. With robotic manufacturing it was easier to custom make everything, and save money by not having a physical shop.

The three of them were sitting at the breakfast table. It was early, and the children hadn't woken up yet. The Sheriff was wearing flannel pyjamas and Frances had a robe over her nightdress. Justine wasn't wearing anything. She saw no need for clothing when she was at home, since she had fur. Clothes were uncomfortably hot and impeded her tail. Victoria's daughter was sleeping over that night. Victoria had previously been their maid, but when the Sheriff discovered she had come into a substantial inheritance, he had elevated her to the status of family friend. As a consequence, babysitting was now unpaid but reciprocal.

Frances wanted to show the Sheriff the online shop's photo-realistic rendering of him wearing the dress she thought he should buy for the interview, but the Sheriff's attention was on his phone.

"I've got an e-mail from the appointments commission! Maybe they've changed the date for the interview."

They all stopped talking.

"Go on then, read it out!"

"Dear Sheriff Cockburn, we write to inform you that our other shortlisted candidate has intimated that she no longer wishes to be considered…"

"YES!" Frances banged the table with joy.

"Shhh!" hissed Justine, "you'll wake the kids!"

"I heard Janice Jamieson, the Sheriff in Glasgow, was offered a partnership in Smith, Smith, Smith and Shitehawk. I wonder if she was the other candidate?" mused Frances.

The Sheriff continued reading.

"The panel have therefore considered your application and qualifications and are able to offer you the position without interview subject to certain requirements…"

"You've got it. Wow! A Supreme Court judge. And soon you'll be a baroness. They always give judges a title."

The Sheriff continued reading.

"As you know, Baroness McPherson represented the judiciary on the Scottish Prostitution Service Board of Management and the Milk and Semen Marketing Board and was also chairperson of the Penitentiary Disciplinary Equipment Committee. The panel feels her successor should continue these roles and therefore we have consulted with these bodies about the appointment."

"Great! Do you think you will be paid extra?" asked Frances.

"Hold on, there's more…"

"Given your recent adoption of a female identity and concomitant lack of experience as a recipient within the female justice system, the employee representatives on these boards raised concerns about your qualifications. Therefore, the appointments committee has decided there should be a professional development requirement of a minimum of ten customer ratings with an average of three and a half stars or better at His Majesty's Brothel, and a minimum of fifty litres of milk produced for the Dairy Farm. Your appointment will initially be for one year on a probationary basis. Baroness McPherson has kindly agreed to continue to represent the justiciary on these committees until the required professional development is complete."

"Should you wish to decline this offer, please inform us as soon as possible so that the position may be re-advertised."

"With Best Wishes, Juan Kerr (Clerk to the Supreme Court)."

They all sat silent for a minute, taking this in.

— ♦ —

Meanwhile in Minneapolis, Claire had a more immediate barrier to her dream of returning to Scotland than the need to take on Baroness McPherson's sentence. Her previous trip with her husband had used up more than half of her 10,000km lifetime air travel allowance. Taking account of the travel she'd done before her Scotland trip, she had less than 2,000km left. Worse than that, under US carbon reduction laws after the previous intercontinental trip, she was banned from intercontinental travel for ten years. She was sure she wouldn't be able to travel from the US to Scotland by air or sea: probably she wouldn't even be able to purchase a ticket, but if she did, she'd almost certainly be arrested and fined at the US border. However, there was no need to travel by air or sea. After decades of global warming, the Arctic regions were far more accessible and there was high-speed rail all the way across what had once been the frozen north. Claire's plan was to travel by rail via Alaska, through the tunnel under the Bering Strait, across Russia on the Trans-Siberian Railway, then from Moscow to Berlin, Berlin to Paris, Paris to the London Underground and finally to Edinburgh on the Flying Scotsman. The first step of her marathon journey was to take the Winnipeg Flyer across the Canadian Border. The distance to Winnipeg was just under the notifiable amount and the only border check needed to enter Canada was a simple identity verification with an iris scan. Once she was out of the country, the miles she racked up would not be reported to the US government as long as she kept each ticketed trip under 500km. The journey was going to take nearly two weeks and consume almost all her savings, even if she avoided the expensive Hyperloop trains. Everything she needed for a four-year stay in Scotland would need to fit in a rucksack and a suitcase on rollers. But it was possible.

While Claire was crossing the green plains of Siberia, absorbed in crafting the denouement of her latest and by far her best wizard related novel, Baroness McPherson was making the arrangements for the honeymoon night in Edinburgh. The Baroness decided to spare no expense on the welcome for the young American given the Brothel sentence she'd be facing and the less than desirable physical characteristics of the husband she'd be accepting. Since the new bride was obsessed with the wizard novels, she booked the suite at the Balmoral where the last of them had been completed for the Honeymoon. It was extortionately expensive, but Supreme Court Justices were well paid and one night would not break the bank.

Since Claire would need to travel light, the Baroness had also rented the wedding dress. Technically, the groom should purchase the rings, but the Baroness did not trust his judgement and had a firm view that the design of the rings should reflect the seniority of the wives within the family. Claire's ring would be a platinum band of the same style as her own but thinner and with a single diamond where hers had three. Her husband's ring for the marriage to Claire would be a plain platinum band of the same style as for his first marriage, but thinner and not as wide.

The final stage of her journey on a steam train from King's Cross Station was the most exciting for Claire. It was disappointing the locomotive was green instead of red and the nameplate read 'Flying Scotsman' but the coaches had compartments and if she closed her eyes, it was easy to imagine she was on the way to wizard school. However, despite the attractions of the train, the most important thing was to finish her novel. Clarie had almost fainted with joy when the Baroness had told her what she'd booked for the honeymoon. She had a chance of adding the final full stop to her work-in-progress in the very room where her hero had completed the final wizard novel! But she was also on a tight schedule. The train would get into Edinburgh Waverley at six am. She could check into the suite in the Balmoral at noon and the Baroness and her new husband would arrive at three pm. It was safe to assume that once the nuptials commenced, there would be limited opportunity for writing. Allowing an hour to get cleaned up and dressed, the writing would need to be finished by two pm. She reckoned she had five thousand words to go. She'd been managing two thousand words a day. It was the most important part of the book and there were now less than twelve hours to write it, assuming she didn't sleep at all.

By the time the train passed the Scottish border at Berwick the villain had met a suitably sorry end - impaled by his broomstick, after carelessly giving the command 'up' at precisely the wrong moment. All that remained was the first and second happy ending scene. But her mind was blank! She was so tired.

Someone was shaking her.

"We're in Edinburgh, miss. Make sure you have all your things and leave the train."

She'd slept for an entire hour.

Fortunately, the hotel was only a short walk away across the station concourse. The desk clerk sniffed and looked at her with something between contempt and disgust, but deigned to check the booking. To be fair, she hadn't showered since Berlin and that was three days ago. The last few days had all been on cheap seats: no sleeper compartments or hotels. The booking could not be denied, but she wouldn't get in the room until noon and it was made clear to her that if she wanted to stay in the hotel until then she'd need to spend money in the cafe or the bar. So she left her suitcase at reception and went out into the streets of Edinburgh in search of somewhere with cheap coffee and Wi-Fi.

She turned right, and headed over North Bridge, figuring that if she wanted cheap, it was best to get a little further away from Princes Street. Memories flooded back as she saw the Castle. The Royal Mile was as picturesque as ever, but again, a bit too expensive for her purposes. So she kept going along South Bridge towards Old College. She remembered the amusement arcade from her previous trip. It had always looked old and dirty and ancient coin-operated games didn't interest her. But it had apparently changed owners. It was brighter now, with stripped wooden flooring and stonework, and as well as gambling machines for the Brothel lottery, there were a few tables and a coffee bar. Best of all, the place was almost empty, and the server was male. In her experience, an empty cafe with a male server meant she had an excellent chance of taking one of their tables and nursing a coffee for hours while she worked on her laptop.

She bought a synthetic-milk latte with a double shot of espresso and a scone for five euros and found a table near enough a wall socket she could plug in her laptop. She reckoned she still had about 3,000 words to go. It was nine am, so three hours here before she could check in. Then maybe two hours in the hotel, before she would need to get cleaned up and dressed in preparation for her new husband's arrival at three pm. She might just manage it.

At two thirty pm, Claire was in the shower when she heard a knock at the door of the suite. Almost immediately there was another knock and the sound of a keycard in the lock. She could hear a male and a female voice.

"I told you not to take your pill until we got here, David!"

"I didn't know it would work so fast. It's the first time I've taken an extra strength one."

"Well, we're early. I said three o'clock and I can hear the shower. Look, there's the wedding dress ready to put on."

"I can't go back downstairs like this! We'll need to go in and wait in the sitting room. We can look at the art."

"Don't worry Claire, it's just Marion and David," called Baroness McPherson. "I'm sorry we're a little early. Take your time!"

But the instruction not to worry was too late. Claire had already dashed out of the shower in search of some clothes. She ran straight into Mr and Mrs McPherson, dripping wet and with only a towel held in front of her to preserve a modicum of modesty.

"Oh, hello! I wasn't expecting you for another half hour. I'm sorry I'm not ready."

Her eye fell on the bulge in the front of Mr McPherson's kilt, which was pushing his sporran to one side.

"I'm afraid he took his pill too soon. I said, take it when you get to the room, but he wouldn't listen. It probably won't last dear, better make the most of it while you can!"

Claire was secretly quite glad she wouldn't need to waste precious writing time fixing her hair and makeup and donning the wedding dress. She still had at least a thousand words to go.

"Pleased to meet you both!" she said. "Maybe we should just do the rings first?"

David fumbled in his sporran and eventually found the jeweller's box. Claire held out her left hand.

"I don't think I should say the 'with this ring, I thee wed' thing," said David, "since technically we are already married, but in any case." He slipped the ring onto her finger above the one from her first husband.

"And here is your ring for David," said Marion. "It is traditional in Scotland that the groom buys both rings."

Claire slipped David's ring onto his finger above the one from his marriage to Marion.

"And now that's taken care of, I really think you two should get a move on. The clock is ticking on that pill!"

Claire's towel had fallen to the floor when she was dealing with the ring. She'd never learned the trick every other woman seemed to know of tying towels, so they stayed in place.

She looked down. Clearly from the state of David's kilt, the situation was urgent.

"I'd just grab the back of the sofa if I were you," suggested Baroness McPherson helpfully.

"Claire, David's a historian," said the Baroness to make conversation while her husband divested himself of his sporran and lifted his kilt, like any true Scotsman he wore no underwear with the kilt, "maybe you've read one of his books?"

"I have!" replied Claire excitedly. "I've read them all! I'm so fascinated by Edinburgh. Just a sec…" she reached round to assist David to find the appropriate passage, "there you go."

"You didn't see a kettle or any tea and coffee, did you, dear?" asked the Baroness. "There must be some in a suite like this."

Claire raised one hand from the sofa to point while steadying herself against her new husband's thrusts with the other.

"I think it's over there."

"Ah yes, excellent, I'll put the kettle on. We can have a cuppa when you're finished, and the biscuits are good too. They've got shortbread, David."

Marion had noticed Claire's laptop open on the desk.

"I wondered if you were a writer when you were so excited about us booking this suite."

Claire gasped as David pulled her hips towards him. Things were definitely moving faster now.

"Yes, uhhh, I'm, ahhhh, writing, uhh, uhhhh, uhhhhh, a novel, ah, ah, ah, ah, ah, about wizards."

She relaxed as her new husband concluded the nuptials and withdrew. Marion was reading from the screen of her laptop.

"Ooh, this is good!"

"It's not finished yet. I'm actually on the last scene and I was hoping to finish it in this suite. You know, because I'm a huge fan and the last wizard book was finished here."

Marion smiled, "well my guess is you won't need to worry about David again for a while. So I'd suggest you take your chance and get back to it! We will have some tea and look at the art and memorabilia."

"Look dear, there's a visitors' book. So many famous people have slept here," said David.

"Madame Valerie Caine, I met her a few times," said the Baroness. "She came to Edinburgh just before Independence. She was the first madame when the Tories privatised the prison and turned it into a brothel. And after that, she was headmistress of the school out by the motorway, 'The Val Caine Science Academy'. The one that shut down last year."

"That's a strange career path, a madame and then a schoolteacher."

"I think she was a teacher first, in an English public school. Then the Tories appointed her to handle discipline in the whips' office. The Viceroy gave her the job in Edinburgh." said Marion, "And look, our latest princess stayed here before the marriage last year."

"I never liked that one."

"You said dear, and I don't dispute that her cakes and singing were very poor. But the prince seemed to like her, and in the end, he's the one who needs to marry her for two years."

"Well, if they're just going to let the prince choose, why bother having a competition? They need to get rid of the Golden Buzzer."

Claire struggled to block out their conversation and focus on her novel. Just a few more paragraphs and the story she'd been working on for more than five years would be complete.

David had found an autographed first edition of one of the wizard novels and her new husband and sister-wife had now settled down on the sofa reading. She longed to join them and handle the precious heirloom herself, but there was work to do.

The sun was setting behind the Castle when Claire typed the last sentence of her masterpiece.

"Finally, they were alone. Harriet reached for the wand hidden beneath her pillow and breathed, 'Erectus Maximus!'"

— ♦ —

After a full night of honeymoon activity, the rented wedding dress and newly bought underwear had been donned and ceremonially removed and all the major possibilities for intercourse between a 75-year-old husband and two wives thoroughly explored. Feeling satisfied that they had properly inducted the new family member, Baroness McPherson crept out of the bedroom. Careful to close the door silently behind her, she ordered a continental breakfast from room service and sat down to check the messages on her phone. She smiled to see there was a sexy one from her new husband and sister-wife in Strasbourg. Not long now until she'd meet them in person. But there was also one from the Palace. That didn't happen often, even to a Baroness. She opened it immediately.

"Dear Baroness McPherson, His Majesty requests your presence at the Palace at your earliest convenience to discuss a matter of great importance. Alastair McDonald, Equerry."

Wow! This was worth waking her husband for, and what a pleasant opportunity to demonstrate the social status of her family to the junior wife.

After an exchange of texts with the equerry, she was advised to dress casually, walk down the Royal Mile, and enter through a side door for breakfast with the King.

"Ah, Baroness McPherson," His Majesty held out his hand in greeting, "I have a matter of great sensitivity to discuss. But before I begin, I would like to remind you of your office as Dame Fellatrix of the Most Noble and Excellent order of the Garter Belt."

As a member of The Most Noble and Excellent Order of the Garter Belt, the Baroness was permitted to use the letters DFKS after her name denoting Dame Fellatrix of the Kingdom of Scotland. The order was more commonly known as the Cum Eaters because of the method of their investiture. Suffice it to say, it involved kneeling before the monarch, but it did not require a sword.

Baroness McPherson was surprised and honoured at the King's request.

"Of course, your majesty. It will be a privilege."

She knelt and licked her lips in preparation.

"Oh, no, I didn't mean that!" Then, sensing her disappointment, the King added, "… or perhaps later… Please, sit, have some coffee."

The equerry served Baroness McPherson coffee in an antique china cup.

"Now, to the facts. The reason I raised your membership of the Order of the Garter Belt is because of your oath of silence. What I am about to tell you is top secret."

"Of course, Sire. My lips are sealed - until you request me to open them."

"Very well. Do you remember the attempted robbery of the vault of the National Library of Scotland around six months ago?"

"I will never forget it, I was in my office only a short distance away when it happened. I heard the shooting and then shouting when one of the guards was hit. Mr Mendoza: a tragic loss. But as you know, Europol deployed their new microwave-based non-lethal threat suppression technology. It proved to be a little more lethal than intended, but two robbers survived and were captured. They were not carrying any loot: presumably, the alarm went off too quickly."

"Yes, indeed. But my belief is the robbers were sent to destroy a document, not to steal valuables, and they may have succeeded."

"What sort of document?"

"This is where we get to the heart of the matter. I believe you have recently undergone a temporary marriage?"

"Yes, Your Majesty, as part of the wife-swap arrangement to facilitate my move to the European Court in Strasbourg."

"Well, I imagine you signed a post-dated, no-fault divorce to end the marriage at the prescribed time and that sealed document was stored in a government vault in Strasbourg?"

"As in Scotland, there is no primary legislation allowing for temporary marriage in France, so it is arranged using post-dated divorce papers."

"Well, for the Scottish Royal Family, such documents are held in an archive within the vault of the National Library of Scotland. As you know, every year the reality show 'Scotland's Next Royal' results in a member of the public marrying myself or one of the princes or princesses for two years."

"Of course, Sire, everyone watches that…"

"It is my belief that the latest princess, who married my eldest son last year, is behind the raid on the National Library. I believe she may have sent mercenaries to destroy the sealed post-dated divorce papers."

"But how could a contestant in a reality show find and hire a team of mercenaries?"

"This is the most serious aspect of the whole sorry business, and one where I regret to say the ambitions of my son may be a contributory factor…" the King paused. Baroness McPherson had the impression he was considering whether to go on.

"I have reason to believe that the winner of that show was, in fact, Princess Mathilda of England who entered the competition by subterfuge and that my son knew this and pressed his Golden Buzzer to ensure her victory. Her singing was poor and her cake in the third round was completely under baked."

Baroness McPherson had to agree.

"The cake was definitely sub standard, Sire - and if I may make so bold, the icing lacked finesse."

"Indeed. You may speak freely here. But there is a more serious aspect to this. You see, should this English princess become queen of England and my son become king of Scotland…"

"A second union of the crowns!" Baroness McPherson was horrified.

"Exactly. And I am informed there have been a series of accidents involving members of the English Royal family. I believe a re-unionist plot is afoot and the attackers at the National Library were English mercenaries!"

"And how can I be of service, Your Majesty? Is this not a matter for the Scottish Government?"

"I wish to resolve this quietly, without destroying the reputation of my son and threatening the institution of the monarchy. I believe the way to do this is to restore the status quo by covertly replacing the papers stolen from the vault with a new set. My son need know nothing: at the end of the fixed period he will be divorced, the English princess can be sent packing and everything will be as it should be."

"You wish me to place forged divorce papers in the official archive?" Baroness McPherson was horrified. "But you must know I've taken leave from the Supreme Court and will be moving to Strasbourg in less than a month. My successor has already been appointed, and I have handed in my security pass. In any case, even as a Supreme Court Justice, I had no access to the vault of the National Library."

"Calm yourself, Baroness," the King smiled. "I only wish for you to have a conversation with your husband. I need to discover as much as possible about the vault and its security. As I understand it, the mechanisms protecting the vault have not been updated since it was constructed a century ago. Because of their age, my people have been unable to find any information about them online. Your husband is a renowned historian of Edinburgh. No doubt he has spent considerable time studying paper documents in the National Library. Perhaps he has seen some relevant historic documents or has become friends with a librarian. We need a starting point."

"Of course, Sire. I shall speak with him immediately on my return."

"All necessary means," replied the King, "the future of Scotland is at stake! And now, Baroness, you may proceed to your other duties."

— ♦ —

Baroness McPherson rushed back to the hotel from the palace and burst straight into the bedroom. Her husband was buried deep in his new wife. Baroness McPherson waved her hands to attract Claire's attention. She couldn't open her mouth in case she lost a little more of the precious cargo she had saved in the fold of her cheek.

"Mmmmmmm," she said.

"You've not!" said her husband.

Baroness McPherson nodded.

She came over to the bed and kissed her husband, then Claire.

"Your mouth tastes of jizz," said Claire.

Baroness McPherson nodded emphatically.

"Royal Jizz?" asked her husband.

Another nod.

"Wow!" said Claire, "my first day in Scotland and I've already tasted the King's jizz. Best. Trip. Ever!"

"It's a solemn moment, Claire. Now you have imbibed the Royal Jizz you must swear loyalty to the King and keep his secrets forever. It's a tradition."

"I'm American. I don't believe in kings and such. But since I'm a McPherson by marriage, I swear, for as long as I'm married to your husband, that I will keep the King's secrets."

"You too, David. You tasted the Royal Jizz as well."

"Of course, I am a loyal Scotsman!"

The Baroness would have liked a bit more permanent commitment from Claire, but it was the best she was going to get.

"David, I need you to tell me everything you know about the National Library of Scotland and particularly the vault under it."

"Well, my books are at home, and…" he looked down at his erection "…I wonder, would you mind waiting a few minutes until I finish."

"Oh… of course, I'm sorry. You two carry on!"

The Baroness waited patiently until they had concluded their business and cleaned themselves up.

"So dear, about the library…"

"Ah, yes. Well, the building itself is only a little over one hundred years old. It dates from the 1930s. Much less historic than the court buildings around it. There is a great deal of mystery about the vault. Almost all the information about it was removed from the public records, although I have seen a few references in old books which were not redacted. Possibly they were missed or, more likely, the librarians did not wish to damage the book."

"So what do these books say?"

"Very little. The vault was constructed at the onset of the second world war. Considerable effort was expended to create a depository secure enough to preserve the Scottish state treasures such as the Crown Jewels and historic documents. It is buried deep in extremely hard igneous rock. Much of the old town is constructed over a lava flow from an ancient volcano. This is why it is so ridiculously expensive for the Council to construct the new tram tunnel…"

"Back to the vault, please David." The Baroness was aware how easily her husband could be diverted from any subject towards complaints about the Council.

"Well, there's not much else to say. It is definitely deep underground. It may be directly under the library or possibly under one of the nearby buildings with a connecting tunnel. The security mechanisms date from the 1930s or 40s and are mechanical in nature. There are no electronic components or computers involved. They have chosen not to update them to preclude a hacking attack or the smuggling of cameras into the vault. Only the three most senior library staff have access to the vault. Probably less than ten people currently alive have ever seen inside."

"So, what does the vault hold?" asked Claire.

"As far as I know, it is used for three separate categories of items. The first is documents deposited with the Copyright Library, which are restricted from public view. Only the most significant of such documents would be stored in the vault because, naturally, space is very limited. The second is particularly sensitive post-dated legal documents such as divorce papers. And the third is national treasures."

"Assuming a thief could get into the vault, is there additional security within it such as locked gates?"

"That, I couldn't tell you. It would seem like an obvious precaution. The person you need to speak to is Bill McLinchie. Bill was the Deputy Chief Librarian when I was researching my first book, but he is long since retired. He's the only person I know who has had access to the vault and who you might have a chance of obtaining information from. He's no fool, but he is old. Perhaps if you are patient and persuade him to indulge in a little single malt whisky, he may let something slip."

"Have you heard anything about the books which are kept in the vault, David?" asked Claire excitedly.

"Not specifically. A book might be restricted because of a complaint of plagiarism or misuse of intellectual property or, more recently, because it offended against one of the political correctness laws. But only the most sensitive examples would merit being kept as a physical book or document in the vault. Most documents are simply digitised and held on the library's computers. Any access restrictions are enforced by encryption."

It was approaching checkout time at the hotel, so they got dressed and packed up their things, but before they left, Marion had an important phone call to make. A honeymoon and an interview with the King were very pleasant distractions. But she was still a convicted criminal with a weekly sentence to serve and with Sheriff Cockburn now promoted into her old position on the Supreme Court, she needed to speak with his successor.

"Hello, Roger? It's Marion." Justice McPherson would not have initiated first-name terms with him when he was a mere procurer fiscal, but since his promotion to sheriff, he was a colleague in the judiciary, albeit a junior one. More importantly, she needed a favour.

"Sorry?"

"Marion McPherson." That didn't work either.

"Baroness McPherson."

"Oh, Good Morning, Justice McPherson. It is an honour. I thought you were on your way to Strasbourg."

"Roger, I have a somewhat delicate situation, which Sheriff Cockburn used to handle for me. I was wondering if you might continue in his place."

The new sheriff knew very well what the situation was, but he had been practising law long enough to know that when you know something about someone which you aren't supposed to know, then you need to feign ignorance until they tell you themselves.

"How can I be of service, Baroness McPherson?"

"This is strictly confidential, Roger…"

"Of course."

"As you know, the wife swapping chain we are both involved in which will take me to Strasbourg also brings a lady from America, Dr Claire Streatham, to Edinburgh to be the second wife for my husband… by the way, has your new wife Madame l'Hôpital arrived from Strasbourg yet?"

"She's arriving tomorrow. My wife and I have booked the honeymoon suite at the Hydro. I thought a bit of country air…"

"Excellent, I wish you all the best! My new husband tells me you are in for a treat."

"…so Marion, how can I help…"

"Well, the thing is, as a result of an unfortunate sentencing error I made some time ago, I received a substantial punishment myself. It was a simple slip up. I accidentally added an extra zero to the fine proposed by the sentencing computer when entering my judgement. However, the prisoner involved had already carried out a significant fraction of her sentence before the error was discovered and bore something of a grudge against me. To cut a long story short, she refused a financial settlement and in her victim impact statement requested that I suffer the identical consequences to herself."

"I see." The new sheriff was pleased that he'd managed to sound appropriately severe at the mention of a criminal sentence.

"In any case, my sentence will be taken over by Dr Streatham to allow me to leave the country and so Dr Streatham will need to surrender herself to the custody of His Majesty's Brothel and have a bracelet fitted. I was wondering if we could handle this privately. Perhaps you could come over for tea and bring the necessary equipment."

"Of course, I'd be delighted to meet Dr Streatham, especially as we are part of the same chain. I'm sure my wife would love to meet her too. She's a very brave lady to take on someone else's sentence and there's no need for any unpleasantness at this stage of the process. We can handle it all informally."

"Excellent. Oh, and Roger, the other small matter about my sentence. Sheriff Cockburn used to handle my weekly punishment. Now you've taken over, perhaps you could bring the… instruments… and we can deal with that this afternoon?"

"Very well, Marion, I shall check your transcript to see what is required and see you this afternoon."

"Come over around four and bring your wife!"

— ♦ —

Sheriff Bellenden and his wife arrived at Baroness McPherson's apartment in Blacket Place at four pm on the dot. One of his first actions on being appointed sheriff had been to purchase a regulation set of punishment instruments from the specialist dealer on Victoria Street. The strap was made by craftsmen in Lochgelly, the canes had been imported from England and the case was the work of the shop itself. Everything was brand spanking new, and he felt that disciplining a Supreme Court Justice was a very auspicious way of christening his new implements. Perhaps, they did not have the same cachet as the previous sheriff's heirloom instruments but, nevertheless, they were far more appropriate for aristocratic buttocks than a standard-issue set from the court stores.

Baroness McPherson and her husband had the ground and garden flat on the left side of a Georgian villa. The Sheriff reckoned a property like that had to be worth at least five million euros. The Baroness showed them through to a sunny conservatory, which opened out on the spacious rear garden and fetched tea, biscuits and a small jug of human milk from the new dairy on Alex Salmond Bridge. Her hospitality did not quite reach to the fantastically expensive tiny jars of semen the dairy also supplied.

Baroness McPherson made the introductions.

"So Roger, you've met my husband, David and this is our new wife Claire… Claire, Roger was recently appointed as sheriff. Sheriff Cockburn was promoted and is now on the Supreme Court."

"Pleased to meet you, sir." Claire was staring at the leather case, which Roger had tactfully pushed under the table.

"And Philomena is Roger's wife…"

"Oh yes, Hi Philomena, I remember your picture from the wifeing.com website, you're in our wife swapping chain, aren't you?"

"Yeah, I'm off to Germany in a few weeks. It's so exciting!"

Philomena sat down beside Baroness McPherson's husband and placed his hand on her knee. She wasn't clear about the extent of the Baroness's invitation: to the Edinburgh middle class 'for dinner' would clearly involve wife swapping, but 'for tea' was ambiguous. In the circumstances, given the Baroness's social status, she thought it polite to show willing. There was an awkward gap in the conversation. Claire was still staring at the leather case.

"Have you got my bracelet in there? Can I see?"

"Oh… no. The bracelet is in my pocket. Here, have a look. Nothing to worry about."

Roger fished in his pocket, took out a jewellery case, and handed it to Claire.

She clicked the clasp open and took it out. The bracelet was of polished black material. She wasn't sure exactly what. It was too cool to be plastic, but didn't feel like metal either. The bracelet hinged open as she lifted it from its case.

"It goes on your left wrist. Be careful…"

Claire snapped the bracelet shut and held her wrist up to admire it. There was a buzz as the bracelet narrowed its diameter until it fitted neatly around her wrist and then a click.

"Oh dear! I was going to say 'be careful not to shut it until you are ready because it won't open again' Well, too late now. We used to need a special tool to lock the bracelets shut on an inmate's wrist, but the new ones have an electronically controlled mechanism."

Claire tugged on the bracelet, but it was locked fast.

"Please don't tug it. Attempting to remove the bracelet is illegal, and you can get an increase to your sentence. It is packed full of sensors. It will report you."

Claire stopped immediately, releasing the bracelet as if her fingers had been burned.

"Well, I'm afraid that's it. You are tagged, which means you are now an inmate of His Majesty's Brothel and subject to all its rules and sanctions. We just need to set up the Brothel App on your phone and pair it with the bracelet so it can access your sentencing details. As soon as your sentence is cleared and you are out of debt to the Brothel, the clasp will unlock and you can take the bracelet off whenever you want."

Claire took out her phone, and the sheriff downloaded the Brothel app and paired it with her bracelet. All that remained was for the biometric sensors on her phone to confirm her identity, after which her phone buzzed and buzzed again as it received a long stream of notifications from the Brothel HR department. She put it back in her pocket.

"So, if it's not the bracelet, what's in your case?"

The Sheriff picked up the long leather case and placed it on the table. Showing a new prisoner the punishment instruments was always a special moment. A little theatre was called for. Even Marion, who'd been a regular recipient for years, had her eyes fixed on the case. He waited for what he thought was an appropriate period for dramatic tension to build, then clicked the metal clasps on each side open. One at a time and then another pause before lifting the lid.

The craftsmen in the back of the shop on Victoria Street had done an excellent job. The presentation case was lined in green felt with a brass plate inset in the middle of the lid inscribed with the names of the manufacturers of each tool. Each one fitted precisely into a custom-designed recess in the felt. At the top was the Lochgelly tawse. The original design dated back long enough to be specified in imperial units. Two and a half inches wide. Three feet long and split into two tongues for the last foot, the width of the tongues gradually tapering to around a quarter of an inch at the tip. It could be used at full length or doubled over according to the desired effect. Then two traditional schoolmaster canes, one thicker than the other. Finally, a small, delicate whip with many light strands of fine leather. And in the lid of the case, sets of leather wrist and ankle cuffs with matching chains.

"They've done a very nice job for you, Roger," said Marion. "Excellent craftmanship and quality materials as usual. When I was a sheriff, I purchased my first tawse from the same firm in Lochgelly. I still have it somewhere."

"It's in the attic, dear. Remember, you hid it away after our tenth wedding anniversary."

Baroness McPherson blushed. "I'm sorry David, but since I got this damned sentence, my buttocks have been in no condition for any further punishment at home!"

"I know dear, I understand completely, but sometimes I miss it."

"We can go and find it after…" interjected Claire and then, realising that talking about what she might do with Marion's husband after Marion left for Strasbourg might be in bad taste, blushed and stopped mid-sentence.

"Let's get it over with, Roger… can you punish me now, then we can all relax. Maybe Claire would like to watch so she can learn the Brothel's procedures."

"Oh, of course. I have your record ready on my phone… here we are…"

"McPherson, Marion. Week beginning 23rd September. Five hours of sex work. Three hours in the Waverley Station glory holes and two hours in the Rose Street red-light district windows."

"What about the corporal punishment?"

The Sheriff checked again.

"Nope. No corporal punishment. There's an annotation on your file… Corporal punishment from this sentence was transferred to inmate Claire Streatham by voluntary agreement."

Claire gasped.

"What! I thought I had two weeks after being tagged before I was on active duty. I read I had to have a special penal MedChip fitted, and allow time for nutrient levels from the Brothel version of Fuel to stabilise."

"Oh dear," said Roger, "I'm afraid the two-week induction period is only for sex work. As soon as you snapped the bracelet shut, you were eligible for corporal punishment. I wasn't expecting you to close it until after Marion had undergone this week's punishment."

"What about the MedChip?"

"Maybe you got one of the new ones when you were in Edinburgh before. They stopped having a special penal version of the MedChip a few years ago and just put the extra circuits for managing prisoners in all of them. These days, pretty much everyone ends up with a sentence sooner or later. I read that fines and license payments from the Brothel and Dairy Farm are now thirty percent of the government's income. There's fewer and fewer people paying income tax, so they need to get the money somewhere. Now you are tagged, they will have activated the penal functions in your MedChip remotely."

Claire turned white.

"The best thing is you come upstairs with me now." said Roger softly, "You're going to have the punishment this week anyway, there's no way out of it, and this way you know who is going to be doing it. In the court punishment booths, you'll have no choice."

"Use the master bedroom, Roger. First door on the left," said Marion, "we'll join you when you are finished."

"It's a pity she's got the new MedChip, I'm sure Roger would have gone easy on her," said Philomena.

Marion shuddered. "I've got a really old one myself. It must be near the end of its lifespan. I've no idea which version they use in France."

"They keep sending me texts to get mine upgraded but I've not gone yet, and in a couple of weeks I'm off to Germany!" said Philomena.

"I hate the whole idea of these new chips. Just imagine getting through your twelve strokes and the computer saying 'Inmate is not yet in sufficient discomfort.'"

From upstairs came the familiar sound of bamboo against skin. THWACK!

Preparations

On her last trip to Edinburgh, Claire had lived in a University grace-and-favour apartment on the Royal Mile. The tram stop on Craigmillar Park was only a short walk from her new husband's home, so Claire caught a tram into town to revisit her old haunts. Only fifty years after the project started the council was close to completing the second line of Edinburgh's tram network. From the University's Bush estate campus south of the city, the line ran to the shopping centre at Straiton, past the Edinburgh National Hospital, Cameron Toll and Craigmillar Park before terminating at the University's George Square campus. The final segment of the line, which was currently being constructed at fantastic expense, would be underground with stops at the Courts and Waverley International before connecting with the East-West tram line on Princes Street.

At Potterrow, Claire's tram entered a concrete sided trench gradually descending from street level to the final 'University' stop, which was underground. Only when she left the tram with the other passengers did she remember she'd not paid for her journey before boarding and she'd left her one remaining working credit card in her rucksack. She saw to her horror that, unlike the above-ground stops, there were ticket barriers at this station. At the barrier there were two lanes, one marked: 'Paid Up' and the other 'Risk It'. Since she had no money, she'd need to go for 'Risk It'. The queue for 'Risk It' was longer than the 'Paid Up' exit because there was a transparent plastic cubicle to negotiate. The barrier forced passengers to enter the cubicle one at a time, and that slowed progress. Above the cubicle was a sign "Edinburgh Trams. Fare dodgers exit. Your chance of being caught is 1 in 20. Fine is 200 euros collected immediately by H.M. Brothel."

The man in front of her in the fare dodger's queue's luck had run out. The cubicle door clicked shut. Customers in the 'Paid Up' queue laughed and clapped as the trapped man pushed against the door in vain. A small robot whizzed across the concourse and docked itself in the space under the plastic cubicle. Latches clicked, and the cubicle rose a centimetre or two above the floor, then the robot slowly and smoothly bore it away. The barrier in front of Claire opened and, with nothing blocking the way, she could walk freely out of the station.

Claire emerged in Bristo Square and turned towards Alex Salmond Bridge and her favourite cafe from her previous stay in Edinburgh. She'd been looking forward to ordering a coffee, people watching and starting an article she intended to submit to a literary journal, but without her credit card, the cafe visit would have to wait. In the US she would just pay with her phone, but now she was in Scotland she would need to link it to a euro bank account to make that work. More seriously, her savings were almost gone after paying for the travel from the US and she'd not discussed money with her new husband.

Claire had the impression that Baroness McPherson was the breadwinner in the family and she was going to Strasbourg. Free accommodation and food were part of the wife swap arrangement, but would she also get some spending money? Or would she have to work? She was aware of her skirt moving against her freshly caned bottom and the unfamiliar bracelet on her left wrist. Maybe she'd need to do more hours in the Brothel just to make ends meet.

She noticed the area had changed since she was last here. To her right in Chambers Street, there was a large excavation. The road was fenced off with NO ENTRY signs warning of fully automated construction equipment. Claire guessed the works were to do with the new tram line: if the line carried on underground from the station she'd just got off at, it would pass under Chambers Street roughly where the excavation was. Greyfriars Bobby was still the same as always but on the right of the bridge the courts complex had expanded with a new 'City Farm' taking the tenement next to the prisoner entrance over. On the bridge itself, the City Farm had opened a cafe, and next to it a restaurant and butcher's shop. Claire stood on the bridge looking down into Merchant Street and the miscreants queuing to enter the courts and City Farm. The Farm staff were wearing light green dresses which buttoned all the way up in front, and the brothel staff were in their navy blue uniform. Claire realised with a shudder that soon she may be in that queue herself. Although, perhaps friendship with the Sheriff would allow her to avoid that indignity.

"Hey! Hello! Dr Streatham!"

Somebody was waving at her. Claire jerked out of her thoughts and looked around to see who it could be. Who would know her name in Scotland?

There were two women in front of her, both five or ten years younger than herself. The one who was waving was wearing combat trousers and hiking boots. Her friend had an elegant dress. Walking just behind the women were an extremely small boy and girl wearing the uniform of Farnon's school. Farnon's was the only school still open in Edinburgh because only the richest could afford a licence to have a child.

"Hey, Dr Streatham! It's Justine."

Claire still couldn't place her.

"I was your maid, remember?"

"Oh, of course, I'm sorry. I didn't recognise you, Justine. You look so different!"

"I know. It's no problem. A lot of things have happened to me since then. This is my son Robert, and my friend Victoria and her daughter Agnes."

"It's a pleasure," said Victoria. "Justine's told me all about you."

The children shook hands dutifully.

"My mummy catches prisoners for the Brothel," Justine's son informed Claire, looking pointedly at the bracelet on her wrist, "so you better not try to run away!"

Justine laughed. "Of course she's not going to run away, darling. Lots of good people have bracelets these days. Even Victoria."

Victoria slid her wrist out of her sleeve a little so Justine's son could see her bracelet, "It's very useful, I can pay for things with it and people can see where I am and come and help me if I get in trouble. Like when I was kidnapped."

Victoria's daughter nodded. "My mummy's good and she's got a bracelet."

Claire was focussing on something else Victoria had said.

"You can pay for things with the bracelet? Really?"

"Of course. You can charge things to your account with the Brothel. As long as you pay the bill promptly, it's just like a credit card. It's convenient and there's often a discount for Brothel employees. Didn't they tell you all this when they put it on?"

"I only got it yesterday. I haven't read all the messages they sent to my phone yet. I'm here on a wife swap with one of the judges in the Supreme Court, Baroness McPherson."

"Yeah, I know," said Justine. "Actually, I was keeping an eye out for you. I thought you'd want to go to the cafe on the bridge where you used to write. I know all about the swap. Remember, I married the Sheriff - well, she got promoted when Baroness McPherson quit to go to Strasbourg. Now she's got Baroness McPherson's job on the Supreme Court."

Claire remembered Justine's husband, the Sheriff, clearly, and he'd definitely been male when she was in Scotland before. But now Justine was referring to her husband as she. Pronouns were a nightmare, when people could change their legal gender by flipping a setting on their phone, and what was worse you could get fined for getting them wrong. The easiest thing was not to say anything if you weren't sure.

Victoria looked at her phone to check the time. The bell would be ringing to start the school day in a few minutes.

"I'll drop the kids off. Get a place in the queue for the cafe and I'll join you." She crossed the road with the children in tow, taking the shortcut to the school through Greyfriars Churchyard.

"We're going to the Milking Parlour," said Justine, "the new cafe in the City Farm. If you've got time, please join us! I'd love to catch up and if you hadn't been brave enough to take on Baroness McPherson's sentence, my husband would never have got the promotion. The least I can do is buy you a coffee with some fresh milk."

"Fresh milk? Really?"

"Yep. As fresh as it gets. Come on, you'll see."

The Milking Parlour Cafe was famous because they prepared their coffee with completely fresh natural milk. The cafe was directly above the milking parlour of the City Dairy Farm and a glass floor allowed patrons to look down onto the gleaming brass pipework and the thick wooden posts to which the cattle would be bound. Since farming animals had been banned under UN carbon reduction laws, only human milk and artificially synthesised milk substitutes were available. Human milk was extortionately expensive and there was always a suspicion that cheaper artificial products may have been substituted. But in this cafe the entire process was visible and you could be confident of getting what you paid for.

Justine and Victoria chose a table in the back room of the cafe. There were no windows, but it didn't matter because almost all the customers were looking down through the glass floor into the milking area. The top of their table lit up as they sat down to provide a touch screen ordering system. Two Columbian roast espressos. Two scones, a small pot of strawberry jam. A small pot of semen and a jug of milk. Two hundred euros. They flicked through the pictures of the cows on offer that morning until they found the ex-sheriff, now Justice Elaine Cockburn. The medication had done its work; the vet had signed off Elaine's milk as fit for human consumption and she'd been ordered to report for her first milking that morning. Luckily, nobody else had selected her, and she was still in the holding pen.

They watched the cattle entrance to the milking parlour intently, waiting to see Elaine being brought in. Off to their right, there was a mumble of discontent from the customers waiting at the to-go queue. The lady attached to the cappuccino machine had run out of milk and they needed to swap over. She was unbuckled from the post and herded away by a farm worker so her replacement could be brought in. When on the farm premises, the penal functionality implemented in the new MedChips was used to block the City Farm cows' ability to talk or make use of their fingers. It was a far more civilised system than the one used in the custodial farm in the country for serious offenders. They had their vocal cords removed and their fingers clipped off.

Elaine was now being herded into the milking parlour and brought to the post nearest to their table. Justine smiled and waved, but Elaine didn't look up. She was focused on the wooden post and the friendly milkmaid waiting to connect her to the equipment. A twist of a knob and the pump sucked the air out of the system and the cups latched into place. The milkmaid placed the tube from the pump into a small silver jug and selected 250ml on the dial. The suction from the milking machine began to release her milk, and the metal jug was filling up. Elaine mooed. But after a while, she got used to the sensation of being milked and relaxed as her aching, over-full breasts emptied.

"Looks like your wife is getting into the swing of it, and we'll have some milk for our coffee," said Victoria.

Claire couldn't contain her curiosity. "So, if you don't mind me asking, what on earth has happened to the Sheriff. He was so masculine."

"He needed to identify as a female to get the promotion at work," replied Justine. "It isn't often that a position on the Supreme Court comes up, and Baroness McPherson is an expert on the same area of law. But there is a requirement for the Supreme Court to remain gender balanced, so he had to file for a female identity to apply. His female name is Elaine."

"But why is she in the City Farm? Surely they pay Supreme Court judges enough they don't need to sell milk. Is she in trouble like Baroness McPherson?"

"No, Elaine's not in any trouble. Baroness McPherson was the judicial representative on the management boards of the Scottish Prostitution Service and the Milk and Semen Marketing Board. Elaine is expected to take on those roles as well and, because she only recently acquired a female identity, the committee put a professional development requirement in their offer. She has to provide fifty litres of milk to the City Farm and obtain ten customer reviews with an average of at least three and a half stars from the Brothel in her first year of employment."

"Wow!" said Victoria, "ten reviews and three and a half stars! That's going to be hard work. You know, you are lucky if one customer in fifty leaves a review, and there's always going to be someone that gives you one star and pulls your average down."

"One in fifty," said Claire, "if you think that's bad, you should try getting reviews for urban fantasy novels on Amazon!"

They'd not finished their drinks, but despite the hefty price tag on their coffee and scones, the waitress was already hovering over the table, ready to pounce and clear it.

"You don't get much time to drink up in this place," observed Claire. "We've hardly sat down and they're already getting ready to chase us out to give the table to another customer. I was in a cafe on South Bridge the other day and I stayed all morning writing for the price of a coffee and a scone."

"Yeah, this is not the place for impoverished writers," said Victoria. "Was it the old amusement arcade you were in? I was meaning to try that. It looks much nicer since it changed owners."

"It's not bad. There's a sign on the wall that says it was the inspiration for the arcade in TDA Online. They don't have any game machines, though, just some lottery terminals and one of those boxes for trapping people who don't pay."

"Can we have the bill?" Victoria asked the waitress, who was now standing directly behind her shoulder.

"It comes to two hundred euros. Pay up or take your chances? You can charge it to your Brothel account, madam."

Victoria smiled.

"No, I'm feeling lucky today. I think I'd rather take my chances."

"Very well. Come this way. The Dishonesty Booth is in the corner. Standard odds of one in ten."

Victoria walked over to the transparent booth in the corner of the cafe. All eyes were on her as it clicked shut. A display showed an animation of a spinning wheel with ten sectors, one of which was coloured red and the others green.

"What's she doing?" asked Claire. "She must be rich to have a kid at Farnon's and dress as she does. Why's she taking the risk?"

"It's her thing," shrugged Justine. "She likes the excitement. Also, she lives off Brothel Fuel. I keep telling her that stuff is dangerous. They say it is a perfect balance of nutrients but I can smell there's more than food in it, and it's been getting stronger."

A minute later, Victoria rejoined them.

"Lucky again!" she said, but she didn't sound like someone who thought they'd been lucky.

"Let's check out this amusement arcade. We've got bracelets, so if it's got a booth, we can ride there on the Inmate Transport System," suggested Victoria.

The Brothel had replaced its guards and prison vans with an automated system using technology developed for warehouses. Prisoners were locked into standard sized transparent containers and moved around the court complex using automated handling. When they needed to be moved between Brothel facilities, flat-bed trucks with a robotic arm loaded up to ten containers for the trip. Displays above every container showed the QR code necessary to order the inmate within. The Dishonesty Booths in tram stations and shops were based on the same standard container. The system was so convenient for navigating the maze of buildings in the court district that staff had taken to using it as well.

"I don't mind using my badge to send you two, but I'm not getting in that thing myself. I'll walk!" Justine's Labrador side refused point-blank to get into one of the small plastic cells, but it loved walking.

Justine pulled her official pass out of her pocket and hung it around her neck. The top of the pass bore the letters PIMP in blue block capitals. Although PIMP was not, strictly speaking, an acronym for Scottish Prostitution Service, Inmate Management Police, the Brothel management had deemed it close enough. She walked to the front of the cafe.

"Brothel PIMP. She held up her ID Card. I need to use your booth." The waitress nodded. It was always fun for the cafe customers to see the booth in action.

"You first!" said Justine in her best tone of authority and pointed at Victoria.

Victoria got into the booth and the door clicked shut.

Justine held her card near a panel on the side of the booth.

"Computer, deliver inmate to South Bridge."

The booth descended through the floor of the Cafe into the City Farm below. Thirty seconds later, another transparent cell arrived.

"Now you!" Justine pointed at Claire, who was soon also on her way.

— ♦ —

Victoria emerged from the Dishonesty Booth in the arcade on South Bridge. She'd walked past it many times but had never been inside. The cafe area was empty apart from a young man behind the bar, who looked thunderstruck. No doubt it was unusual for the booth in a cafe to deliver someone rather than take them away, but surely not unusual enough for that expression. Victoria wondered if her company owned this property. Maybe he was scared because he'd recognised her as the owner of Argyle Investments and he'd done something forbidden by the lease.

"Hello there!" she said.

"Hello...I thought you were only in the game," stammered James.

The woman who had stepped out of the booth in his arcade was without question the same person he had met in Echo Park and who had sent the money. He'd remember her face anywhere. He'd assumed the woman in TDA was one of the Guild's resurrected consciousnesses, but here she was in the real world. She must have created a game avatar with an exact model of her own face.

Victoria was aghast: this man had said he'd seen her face in the game world. It was a disaster! Victoria had made it clear to the original owner of this face that she expected exclusive use of it and up to now there'd been no inkling that agreement was being broken.

Then it clicked what the young man must mean. Relief swept over her.

"You mean, on the game?"

"Yeah - that. On the game. I got your money and I've been working hard…"

Victoria smiled. "Sorry, I'm off duty". She held up her bracelet to show him. But the display on her bracelet was illuminated in yellow and read 'For Hire.' At first, she'd no idea how her status had changed without her using the app on her phone, but then she realised that it probably happened automatically when she used the Inmate Transport System. It made sense for prisoners being moved around the courts and brothel facilities. In any case, the rules were strict: if your status was set to 'For Hire' you needed to accept bookings.

"You're right, I am on the game. Let's wait for my friend and then we can go somewhere more private."

Behind her, the empty cell was lowered down through the floor to make space for the one containing Claire. Claire's bracelet was also illuminated when she stepped out of the transparent cell.

Claire recognised the man who'd served her when she was writing in the arcade two days before and gave him a friendly smile.

"Is there a secret underground area in this arcade, like in the game?" she asked.

James was still distracted by Victoria, but he turned to Claire.

"Not really. I'm told there is a secret space under the bridge and that's what gave them the idea, but I don't think it is accessible from the arcade. There is a Manager's Office though."

"Can you show us? I used to play TDA a lot when I was young," asked Claire.

James looked at Victoria. There were a lot of secrets in that office, but it was her 30,000 euro that had paid for the whole setup.

"If it's OK with your friend, I can show you around."

Victoria had no idea why this man was asking her permission, but couldn't see a reason not to say yes.

"Sure."

James went over to the front door, locked it, and turned the sign over to 'Closed' to ensure privacy while he was giving his investor a tour.

"So this is our main space. I threw out the old carpet and stripped back the walls and floors to show the original stone and wood. The machines you can see are owned by the Brothel. They rent the space for their lottery terminals and Dishonesty Booth from the arcade. There are some old coin-operated machines the previous owner left behind downstairs. I'm hoping to repair some of them and get a few newer ones myself. Maybe a virtual reality area mapped to the arcade in TDA. Then we have the cafe, and I've got some legal pharmaceutical teas and cakes. We get Brothel employees using the booth to access the Inmate Transport System, so I started to cater to that market with anaesthetic liniment and so on."

"Do you have tequila?" asked Claire.

James smiled.

"Not yet, my drinks licence hasn't come through."

"If I was an NPC in the game, I think I'd be the girl who works in the arcade. I'd drive the players around in a van like the one in Scooby-Doo. It would be off the radar because I'm an NPC and I could bring back the equipment for the heists, so players don't need to make two trips. Maybe I could have a heist planning board in the back of the van too, so they wouldn't need to go back to the arcade after every prep mission."

This was a girl after James' own heart!

"You're right, the other buildings have special vehicles, the arcade should too! A Scooby-Doo van would be great," said James. "Come on, I'll show you the office."

"That's cool," said Claire, "you've got an arcade machine in the Manager's Office just like the game. Have you got, a secret planning room too?"

James looked at Victoria but she didn't give any sign that he shouldn't show Claire the planning room.

The machine was on casters so he simply lifted the latch which locked the wheels in place and pushed it to one side. It was a lot less impressive than the mechanism in the game, but also a lot less expensive.

Now it was Victoria's turn to be astonished. She stepped through the narrow access hatch into a low ceilinged room with three computerised whiteboards covered in drawings and photos which looked like planning for a robbery. On a large video screen, somebody who looked exactly like a character from TDA Online was standing in the arcade in the game, holding a marker pen in front of his own copy of the three whiteboards.

"Milton Mowbray," she breathed, "you're alive!"

Claire walked straight over to the planning boards and stared at them. "It's just like in the game!"

"Claire, we're leaving. We've made a mistake!" hissed Victoria. Nothing good could come of this.

"Hire them!" shouted Milton. "Hire them both, right now, on your phone, quick!"

James grabbed his phone, his thumb moving fast over the screen. Before she reached the door, Victoria's bracelet flicked over to 'Engaged' and a second later, so did Claire's.

"Now ladies," said Milton, "you have been hired as Brothel employees. Which means…"

"I know, we are bound by the Brothel NDA and can't say anything to anyone about what we have seen here," replied Victoria, "don't worry, we are leaving and your secret is safe."

The Brothel's Non-Disclosure Agreement ran to thirty-seven pages of tight legal text and the penalties it specified were both inventive and Draconian.

"Not so fast. James here just paid you for your services. I expect he will want his money's worth. But first, I want to know why you have the same face as Dr Roberta Knox's character in TDA Online!"

Victoria was relieved. If Milton thought she was Roberta Knox, he was barking up completely the wrong tree. Was Milton just guessing that the avatar which looked like her was being played by Dr Knox, or did he have firm evidence? As far as Victoria knew, Dr Knox had never even seen this face. As an artificial life form, Milton was an unknown factor. He could potentially be much less or much more intelligent than a human.

Claire was still staring at the planning boards, oblivious to their conversation.

"If you guys are robbing the vault of the National Library of Scotland," she said, "I want in."

"They're doing what!?" asked Victoria and went to have a closer look at the boards herself.

At this point, Milton would have preferred to tie his visitors up and threaten them until he found out who they were. The problem with this plan was that James was as weak as wet toilet paper and he felt sure the woman from Echo Park was not to be trifled with. There was a reason the first mission on any heist should be acquiring unmarked guns.

"So, Mr Arcade Man, I'm Victoria and this is Claire. What's your name?" asked Victoria. "You may as well tell us. You've leased the arcade, it will be on all kinds of documents." There was no point in hiding her name. He'd have got it off the Brothel app when he booked her, anyway.

"James," he said, "James Miranda Fergusson. And the character in the game is Milton. This is all under NDA, remember!"

"Hello Le…" said Claire to the man on the computer screen.

"You're not a million miles away there, but no. I'm Milton Mowbray."

James Fergusson. Victoria vaguely remembered that name. She'd heard it before, in her previous life. That was it: James Fergusson was Dr Knox's PhD student and ran errands for the Guild. And apparently, he'd cooked up a plan to rob the National Library with her old experiment in artificial life. But why? And how had he found Milton?

"So why do you want to rob a library, Milton? Isn't a bank, or a casino more your style?"

"Wouldn't you like to know?" said Milton, tapping the side of his nose.

"They're after the source code to TDA 6," said Claire. "Look, he's drawn a picture of the target on the first board."

"Damn!"

Victoria understood at once. Dr Knox and all the other resurrected Guild members now living in the game world would pay anything for that source code. If the rumours were true, it would expand their world to include multiple cities, every building on the map could be entered, apartments could be fully customised with furniture, the windows on the cheaper apartments would work and there'd be new clothing, new hairstyles and new vehicles. It was no wonder they were trying to acquire it and Victoria was all in favour of them doing so since someday she might need to move to the game world herself. However, helping Milton steal the source code was one thing. Turning it over to whoever was using her face was quite another.

"Don't your plans usually need four people, Milton?" she asked. "Are you really going after the National Library of Scotland with just a low level player like James?"

"Hmm. I've not got to the final board yet but, you are right, we will need a team of four for this operation. And higher level players would make success more likely. Can you fly a helicopter? Or hack?"

"I can't fly a helicopter. It's a lot harder in real life than in the game. But I'm not a bad hacker. If I come in, what's my cut?"

"You know the drill. James is the host. He sets the cut on the last board."

"I'll do it for fifteen percent and I'll help with preps, James," said Claire, "but I'm even lower level than you and there are still only three of us. We should ask Baroness McPherson."

"Baroness McPherson is a Supreme Court Judge," said Victoria. "Are you crazy?"

"I happen to know that the Baroness has her own reasons for wanting to get into that vault. If we help her, she might be able to give us information, and she'll probably not want a cut of our take. Also, she's no goody two shoes, she's got an absolutely massive sentence from the Brothel herself. I've got to take it over when she goes to Strasbourg and I already had the first dose. This week it is twelve strokes of the cane and five hours of sex work, and she's been getting punished like that every week for the last ten years."

"Bloody hell!" said James. "That's hardcore. But we should hire her, so she's covered by the Brothel NDA before we say anything to her."

"Well, you will need to hurry because she will be off to Strasbourg in a week."

They heard knocking from above and checked the monitors for the CCTV system. James nearly had kittens when he saw Justine peering through the front door.

"Don't worry, it's just our friend," said Claire.

"She's a cop. I remember her from when I was sent to the punishment booths in the court. And she's wearing a PIMP badge," said James.

"She's not a cop any more," said Victoria. "She has her own business as a Sheriff's Officer. The Brothel gave her a badge so she can catch runaways for them but she's got some huge case about recovering stolen property and she's not worked on anything else for months."

"Whether she's a cop or a bounty hunting Sheriff's Officer, she's got a PIMP badge, and you are supposed to be running a coffee shop and arcade. You need to lock up the planning room and go up there and make coffee." said Milton.

— ♦ —

The next day, James hired Marion as an escort using the Brothel app. She turned up for the appointment to the arcade just after closing time and James showed her through into the office. Marion got a shock when she saw Claire was there, too.

"You didn't say anything about a threesome!"

Claire grinned. "No, it's not that. The escort booking is only so everything we discuss is covered by the Brothel NDA."

"You don't need to worry about me breaking that NDA. It is fearsome!"

"James and and his friend Milton are planning to rob the National Library of Scotland. I told them you might be interested."

"I'm a judge, not a robber," said Marion pointedly, "but I am interested in finding out about the vault under the library and I might be willing to trade information."

James opened the hidden entrance to the planning room. When she saw the digital whiteboards and the creepy looking master criminal hiding away behind a video link Marion had to admit it looked like a professional setup.

"OK then," said Milton, "what do you have to trade?"

"I can tell you a little about the library," said Marion. "The Historical Crimes and Grievances Division of Police Scotland is located there and I often have business in their office."

"Told you Marion would be useful!" said Claire.

"Start from the main door, and describe what we would see," said Milton.

"Well, the main door is right in the middle of the building on Alex Salmond Bridge. It's just an ordinary wooden door, and it's open during the working day."

"No wonder the robbers could just run in."

"The new security measures installed after the robbery attempt start immediately you enter the building. There is a screen of bulletproof glass right across the entrance lobby with a remotely operated door in the middle. A little further on in the lobby there is a second screen of bulletproof glass which also has a door. Between them is an airport-style automated screening station. The outer door is opened for one person at a time, then locked behind them. The inner door is not unlocked until the screening for weapons, explosives and other contraband is complete and the person has been identified with an iris scan and authorised to enter. The inner and outer doors are never both open at the same time. There's no way a team of armed people could just run through into the library anymore."

"We'd need to use explosives, just to get in the door," said Milton.

"They also have additional armed guards on patrol inside the library. If you got in, there would be more resistance."

"OK, so describe the basic layout of the place."

"Well, the building was designed as a reference library. Originally, there was a foyer with a small cafe and exhibition space which was open to the public and then upstairs there were reading rooms and study spaces. The reading rooms were only accessible with a library card and whatever material you wanted was brought to you there by library staff. Most of the books were stored offsite. They had a van shuttling to and fro, bringing the books people had requested to the reading room and returning them after they were done."

"So it wasn't a proper library with old wooden bookcases and a restricted section with strange and unusual books," said Claire disappointedly.

"The whole library was restricted. You couldn't get anything without proving your identity and making a written request," said Marion.

"But, it's not a library now, it was taken over by the Historical Crimes and Grievances Division of Police Scotland. How did things change?" asked Milton.

"Police Scotland leased the upper floors in the National Library building, and the reading rooms became offices for the investigators in the Historical Crimes Division. The National Library still owns the building, provides the librarians and the offsite book storage and manages the vault."

"So if there are police in the building, why didn't they fight back during the previous robbery?"

"It's the Historical Crimes and Grievances Division. Their investigators are all historians. They never arrest anyone, never mind fight armed robbers."

"Could you describe the path from the front door to the vault?"

"I rarely go through the front door. There's a staff door between the library and the court buildings at the rear, and I use that. They upgraded the security on that entrance too after the robbery."

"OK, can you describe the path from the staff door to the vault, then?"

"I always go straight from the staff door up the stairs to the Historical Crimes Division offices. I don't know how to get to the vault. Most of the ground floor is restricted to library staff. After the robbery, they closed access to the public lobby so my bet is the stair down to the vault is somewhere near there."

"It looks like getting in through the library is going to be difficult. Maybe we should consider tunnelling in from somewhere with less security," said Milton.

"I thought we'd want to find out more about the vault, so I hacked into the Council planning department last night," said Victoria. "All I found was a note that said 'Plans transferred to National Library of Scotland for secure storage. National Security: No electronic copies to be made.'"

"So the only plans for the vault are in the vault?"

"It looks that way."

"Well, that's a problem."

"I'm on the Scottish Prostitution Service Board," said Marion, "we had to approve the building works for the Inmate Transport System and I saw plans of the court buildings and the ground under them. There was a large crosshatched area under the library marked `Redacted, National Security` and also an area marked off for `future tram tunnel`. We weren't allowed to build anything underground in the area under the library or the area reserved for the tram tunnel."

"In theory, we could use sonar to find the vault, like geologists do to locate oil under the ground," said Victoria. "We'd need to set off an explosion and have seismometers buried to capture the resulting sound waves. If we did it properly, it could give us a reasonable 3D map of what's under the library."

"That's all well and good, but we can't just set off explosives in the middle of a city," said Claire, "and we aren't going to get permission to install seismometers all over the place either."

Nobody said anything. It was obvious she was right.

"Actually, the Council already placed sensors in the court buildings to monitor vibration from the tram tunnelling work. They probably put them in the cellars of all the older buildings near the tunnel, not just the court ones. If you can hack into the Council, maybe you don't need to place your own seismometers," said Marion. "Doesn't solve the problem of setting off an explosion without getting arrested though."

"It's a pity we didn't think of this last month," said James, "the explosion when they demolished Henry Dundas's statue must have made some good sound waves."

Victoria's brow furrowed for a minute, then she grinned broadly, "Nobody ever deletes data! If the Council's seismometers were there last month, the data from them will be sitting on a server somewhere. I just need to hack that server and process the data from the time the statue was blown up! Give me a week or two."

"Marion, you are a genius!" said Milton. "I don't suppose you know anything about the security inside the vault?"

"I'm afraid I can't help there," she replied. "The only lead I have is the name of a former head librarian. He's one of the very few people still alive who has seen inside the vault."

"Hold on, what's this old guy's name?" asked Victoria.

"William McLinchie."

"Not Big Bill McLinchie?"

"I was told William, but it's possible he has a nickname."

"I know Big Bill McLinchie." said Victoria, "The McLinchies are a lovely old couple. He was my first customer after I came back from maternity leave. It was his birthday and Mrs McLinchie booked me as a present. She's getting on a bit and her bones are brittle. The doctor said it wasn't safe for her to have sex with him anymore."

"That'll be why he's called Big Bill?"

"Exactly. The Madame gave the booking to me because I'd had a baby and would be less likely to lose my nerve. There had been a previous incident where one of the girls had fainted."

"So, does he ever talk about the library?"

"Oh, yes. You've got to remember he must be at least eighty. People of that age like to talk about things that happened a long time ago more than things that happened last week. He has a lot of stories about the library but I'm not sure all his memories are reliable. Mr McLinchie is a proper gentleman, very honest and loyal to his old employer. If we tried to bribe or threaten him, I'm sure he would report it."

"Do you think I could meet him? I love librarians. He must have seen some amazingly rare books," asked Claire.

"You can take over my next booking, but it is at your own risk. It will have to stay in my name, though. The Brothel wouldn't allow him to book you."

"It's OK, I don't care about the money."

"Fair enough. I'll call him."

"You know, the librarians are not the only people who have seen inside that vault," said Milton. "There's also the two robbers that got caught. They were there more recently, and they will be more open to bribery than the librarian. Is there any chance of talking to them in prison, Marion?"

"They were transferred to the new ultra-max long term storage facility," she replied. "That's where we send the worst of the worst now that the Factory Farm isn't available. The problem is that the price negotiated with the McLeod Corporation to store ultra-max prisoners is based on an agreement that they will never be released. No appeals, no parole, life means life, no in-person visitors, just video calls for immediate family. It makes the security arrangements much simpler and allows the facility to be almost completely automated."

"Jesus!"

"Every aspect is compliant with the Human Rights laws. The average stay is quite short because most prisoners request euthanasia as soon as they realise there is no possibility of release."

"So the robbers, are they still inside?"

"The two surviving robbers are denied euthanasia until they provide a full account of who they are, who sent them and what they were after to the Scottish Government. They are also denied family video conferencing. As the judicial representative on the Scottish Prostitution Service Board, I had to check their conditions, I had a video conference once a month and asked if they were being treated well and were ready to make a statement, but all they ever said was 'No Comment'. They look healthy enough, but it was all very bleak. They never leave a blank concrete one-person cell with a platform for a bed and a small outside area for exercise.

Their only recreation is an ancient video game machine in their cell. The video feed is unusual because the prison runs facial recognition and displays their inmate barcode identifier above their head, but the strangest thing is the hats they make them wear."

Milton perked up at once. "What kind of hat?"

"Pointy hats, like the Dunce Caps they had in schools more than a hundred years ago."

— ♦ —

Claire knocked on the door of the McLinchie Residence at one o'clock sharp that Sunday afternoon. As a visual aid to get his reminiscences flowing, she'd acquired a dress and coat from the vintage clothing shop near the University. She looked like a young female employee of the National Library at the time when Mr McLinchie was a junior manager.

An elderly woman with a welcoming smile opened it. She ushered Claire into the hallway and called to her husband.

"The lady from the Brothel is here, dear!"

"Hello Mrs McLinchie, I'm Claire. My friend Victoria couldn't make it today and she asked me to fill in for her. I hope you don't mind."

"Go straight up, love. Victoria called us and explained. He's in his office, top of the stairs and first on the left. I got him ready for you to save time. I'll get the kettle on. We can have some tea when you're done."

Mr McLinchie's office was a large, high-ceilinged room with a view over Queen Street Gardens. The walls were lined with floor-to-ceiling fitted bookcases filled with an eclectic mix of real paper books. There was a comfortable armchair for reading and an impressive polished wood desk. The original wooden floorboards of the Georgian tenement had been sanded and polished, and an antique Persian rug covered the area in front of the fireplace. Claire could smell the books as soon as she entered the room. It was the second most wonderful room she'd ever been in. First place, of course, was the suite in the Balmoral where the last wizard book was finished.

Mr McLinchie was sitting behind his desk. Claire walked over and immediately saw why he was called Big Bill McLinchie. It was only slightly longer than normal size, but the width was prodigious. She grasped the edge of the desk to steady herself.

"I'm not sure I can manage that!"

"Just relax and take it slowly," advised Mr McLinchie. "I'm sure you will be fine."

Mrs McLinchie knocked on the study door when they were finished and entered, bearing a tray with tea and homemade cake.

"I heard you finishing up, so I brought the tea," she smiled, "that was a very professional job, young lady."

"It was my pleasure!"

"I always say it is his best feature. Many hours of fun I've had from it, but the doctor says that now I am old my bones are getting brittle and I need to be careful and leave it to younger women. Something that size might fracture my pelvis."

She poured the tea and cut the cake.

"So, tell us about yourself, Claire. You sound American. Victoria said you've just come to Scotland on a wife swap, and you're married to David McPherson for four years. It's a small world, you wouldn't believe it, but Bill remembers your husband from when he worked in the library!"

"I teach Intelligent Design and Dance at the University of Minnesota, but I want to be an author. I was in Edinburgh a few years ago with my husband when he did a sabbatical at the University and I jumped at the chance when the opportunity came up on wifeing.com. "

"But what about the carbon laws? How did you manage to travel twice so quickly?"

"I had to come by train. The long way round via Alaska. There were no intercontinental stages in my journey, so I never had to declare it."

"If they find out, you're going to be in trouble!"

"I know. But coming back to Edinburgh was worth the risk, even if they add another fine to my sentence. I had to take on Marion's - Baroness McPherson's - sentence so she could swap with a woman in Strasbourg and join the European Court."

"I heard about that. A tough break for Marion. But I can see why someone who got fined ten times as much as they should have been would insist on the judge getting the same punishment," said Mr McLinchie.

"I'm so interested in the library, I'd have loved to go there. It's a shame they moved the reading rooms out of the old building so the Historical Crimes police could have it. I'm sure there are some stories you can tell. Did you work there too, Mrs McLinchie?"

"No dear, I was a schoolteacher. But I used the reading room in the library when I was at university and that's how I met Bill. I left a food stain on one of the old books."

"I still think you did it on purpose."

"No, it was just a mistake, but I shouldn't have had food in the reading room. Anyway, I'd been eating, even though it was forbidden, and I left a smudge in the margin of a Joanne Rowling novel."

Claire was shocked.

"But you should have been wearing cotton gloves to handle a treasure like that!"

"Yes. Although, to be fair, she was less revered in those days. Anyway, when I handed the book back, the librarian noticed, and I was taken to William's office. He wasn't Big Bill McLinchie then, of course, that happened later as the result of participating in some questionable medical research. The idiots thought they'd isolated the messenger protein which made the penis grow longer during puberty, but they'd actually found the one which made it wider. Not that I am complaining."

Mr McLinchie smiled at the memory.

"In those days, the library could hand out fines. She should have received a hundred euro fine for damaging that book. But I gave her another option…"

Mrs McLinchie grinned. "Show her dear…"

He opened the right-hand top drawer of his desk and took out a leather strap.

"The very next week, she damaged another book and was back."

"I wouldn't damage a book on purpose. I just found a book that was already marked and said it was me."

"Three months later, we were married!" said Mr McLinchie.

"That's such a romantic story! In my book, I'm writing a scene where the librarians have sex up against the bookcases, in the restricted section. Did you ever do anything like that?"

Mrs McLinchie laughed.

"I did worse than that, dear. One time I had sex in the vault!"

"You did what!?" interjected Mr McLinchie incredulously.

"Don't you remember the time at the staff party when we wife-swapped with your boss?"

"He took you down to the vault? That's against all the rules. He could have lost his job for that."

"I asked him to. I wanted to see down there and you were such a stickler for regulations. He finally said he'd show me the vault, but we couldn't go all the way inside. Not a very fair deal, come to think of it. I should have told him the same!"

"That must have been so exciting. What was it like?" asked Claire.

"Well, we went to the ground floor and there was a guard standing beside an unmarked wooden door. He unlocked it, and we went down a flight of steps into the basement. We were in a large room with a marble floor. In the middle of the floor, there was a mosaic with a heraldic crest. I remember there was a Saltire and a Unicorn and an open book. There were metal bars all the way across the room just a little way back from the entrance, with a gate in the middle. On the other side of the bars, there was a guard sitting at a desk facing the entrance. He was wearing body armour and had a gun belt with a pistol. There was a helmet and military rifle within easy reach and a steel plate attached to the bars next to his desk he could take cover behind. The Chief Librarian told him to unlock the gate and take a fifteen-minute break."

"You really shouldn't be talking about Library security," put in Mr McLinchie, "but I know you're going to ignore me anyway, so go ahead."

"So that was it, just an iron railing and a guard, and you were in the vault?" asked Claire.

"Oh no, not at all. Right in front of us, a few metres from the railing, was the actual vault door. The whole wall was shiny, like steel, and the door was set right in the middle of it. It had two locks for keys and a combination dial and there was a big wheel to spin to open it - just like in the movies!"

"Wow! What was it like inside the vault? Did you see any famous books?"

"That's as far as I got. He said we couldn't go any further. It took three librarians to open the vault, two deputy librarians had the keys for the two locks and as the Chief Librarian he knew the combination."

"So what happened then?"

"Well, naturally, he had his way with me. It was a wife-swapping party, after all. There wasn't much furniture down there, so I just grabbed hold of the railings and bent over for him. I still remember I was looking forward straight at the safe and the maker's nameplate above the combination lock. It said `JaS McTear, Banker's Engineer. Springburn Safe Works. 1941.`"

"That's quite enough!" interjected Mr McLinchie, "everything about that vault is a state secret. You should know better, dear!"

"I'm sorry," Mrs McLinchie grinned. "You can spank me later if you want. But you don't need to worry about Claire telling, she's from the Brothel. Everything we say is under NDA."

A shiver ran down Claire's spine at the mention of the Brothel's NDA. She'd been so unnerved after Clause 47c she couldn't read any further and there were still another 20 pages of text and ten pages of full-colour illustrations.

— ♦ —

One of the downsides on living in the arcade and sleeping on a camp bed in the office was James couldn't get away from Milton.

"James, I've got a task for you."

"Why me? Ask one of the others!"

"Are any of the others gamers who used to run errands for the Guild?"

"Well, I'm pretty sure Marion isn't a gamer, and that Claire doesn't work for the Guild. I wouldn't place bets on Victoria."

"Did you recognise what Marion was talking about a few days ago?"

"With the prisoners? Yeah. Those guys are dead and uploaded and put in the prison in TDA Online. They are in a Bad Sport lobby too."

"And uploading people means the Guild."

"It means Guild technology, not necessarily the Guild. Maybe one of their new scanners was left behind when they left, and the government got its hands on it. But I agree, they are uploading prisoners to the prison in the game. It's probably to save money, it must be expensive to feed and guard a violent person for fifty years. People like that used to be sent to the Factory Farm, but that got stopped by the European Court. If they can do a video link from the game and the prisoner doesn't even know they have been uploaded to a computer, they don't need to keep them alive in the real world."

"We need to talk to them. They were inside the vault, they have the information we need and they won't think twice about trading it for a way out of jail. Which means your game character needs to break into Victorville Penitentiary."

"And why can't you do it?"

"Because whoever does this needs to get put in Bad Sport. In case you haven't noticed, I look like one of the most famous NPCs in the game because my creator was lazy and copied a character model that was already in the game rather than using the character editor like a new human player. One look at me and my stats and Polaris Customer Service will ban me for modding. I've got ten years of 24/7 play on this character and I don't want to get reset, but the thing that really scares me is that, if my character gets banned and my neural network can't connect to the game, I will have no sensory input at all."

"OK. Hold on, I'll log in."

"The first step is to get put in Bad Sport. Get a helicopter and blow up some players' cars."

"Just about every noob has a menu or is in God Mode these days," grumbled James, "it's getting to be so you can't even grief a level four player without getting chucked halfway across the map and turned into a giant orange or set on fire."

It took James about an hour to blow up enough personal vehicles to be put in Bad Sport.

"OK, so from what Marion said, the gamer tags look like barcode inmate IDs. I'll look their barcodes up on the Scottish Prostitution Service system. OK, '||.|||||.|.....||||..|||||', is the first one, try to join their lobby."

James's character spawned into his arcade in the new lobby.

"I don't see them on the player list."

"Probably because the area in the prison they are holding them is off the map. You're going to have to steal a prison bus."

"Not again! Can't I just buy one?"

"Buying the bus won't get you the guard's uniform. You've got to start a legitimate mission which involves stealing a bus and breaking into the jail."

"OK, OK! Here we go."

"Right, get a motorbike, catch up with the bus and do a drive-by on the driver."

"No way. I'm going to get a helicopter and land in front of it and shoot the driver as the bus comes towards me."

"If you miss, the bus will get past you and by the time you get another vehicle and catch up again, it will be halfway across the map."

Ten minutes later, and after chasing the bus most of the way to Los Espíritus.

"OK, you were right, but I've got it now."

"Drive to the prison. Then go off the mission script, sneak into the yard and across to the cell block."

"Which cell block?"

"You're going to have to check them one by one."

James drove the prison bus into the jail and parked next to a SWAT van. There was no way to drive the bus into the yard, the gap between buildings was too small.

"Remember, no weapons and don't stay in the guard's cones of vision too long."

"I hate this mission. One slip and it is world war three. They've got Olympic standard NPC marksmen in every tower and police spawning everywhere."

"Stop complaining and go to the door to the first cell block."

"It doesn't open. Just an inactive building."

"You need to glitch it, select a pistol, move right up to the door and aim…"

"Like I was stealing gold in Cay…"

"Yeah. Like that."

James fell through the door. He was in an open hall inside the prison building. There were cell doors on the left and right of the central space and a staircase leading up to a landing with more cells.

"I'm in."

"Marion said their cells have a small outside area for exercise so they must be on the ground floor. See if you can find them."

"I've got no idea what they look like!"

"They'll be the ones with the melted faces. Even in TDA, not many people have had their skin microwaved."

All the cells were full, but, as Milton had predicted, there was no difficulty at all in recognising the prisoners he was looking for.

"Who are you?" asked the first prisoner as he slid back the cover over the view port on the cell door. He was wearing an orange jumpsuit and had a strong accent, like an English servant in one of the costume dramas on the History Channel.

"I'm the guy who can get you out," replied James. "I've got a deal for you. Tell me how you got into the vault and what you saw when you robbed the National Library of Scotland and I'll unlock your cell."

"What use is unlocking the cell. I saw this place on the way in. There's no way I'd get past the fence."

"I've got a prison bus. If you make it to the bus without setting off the alarm, you can drive out with me."

The man considered his options for a minute.

"I'm not a grass, I don't talk to coppers."

"I'm not a cop. I took the uniform off the cop I killed to get the prison bus. Look, you can see some of his blood on the shirt. I'm on a deadline here, there's a prison bus outside with a body in it. Are you going to tell me about the library?"

"OK, I'll talk."

James' character pulled a beer out of its inventory.

"Tell me from the beginning."

"We were in the nick in London. Got caught robbing jewelry from a banker's house and they were saying we'd swing for it. The Tories like their public executions. But this gent from the government offered us a pardon and a lot of money if we did a job for him."

"What gent?"

"No idea. Posh accent, expensive suit, top hat. The jail let him come and go as he pleased so he must have been government."

"OK. So what happened then?"

"There were four of us. They took us out and put us on a train to Hereford. Brought us to an army camp. We were still under guard, but they taught us to use guns and explosives. They had a mockup of the building we were supposed to rob, from the front door down to the vault and we had to practise on it every day until we could get down to the vault in less than two minutes every time."

"What about your escape route?"

"They didn't have a mockup for that and we didn't practice. They just said go out the back of the library, there's a staff entrance to the courts, run through the courts and come out on Parliament Square and there will be a fast car and driver waiting."

"OK, so what happened then."

"When they thought we were good enough, they took us to the Scottish border, and we joined up with some cheese smugglers. We walked for weeks through the forest until we got to the outskirts of Edinburgh. The smugglers left us in the woods not far from the end of the tram line. Bush Estate, it was called. One of the cheese smuggler's mules was carrying our food, guns and explosives, a tent and new-fangled clothes so we would fit in. We had to do the job on a specific day, and we had a couple of days to kill in the tent until it was time. The strange thing was we weren't supposed to nick anything. We were to tear up a document and eat the pieces. Don't burn it, they said, and don't leave a single piece behind. It needs to disappear completely or you don't get paid and you don't get your pardon. Tear it up small and eat it."

"Did they say what the document was?"

"Yeah, it was post-dated divorce papers. They wanted it gone so the divorce wouldn't happen. They didn't tell us who's divorce papers and if they had, I'd have skipped town before I went in that vault!"

"So, what was the plan?"

"We walked out of the woods and took the tram to the stop nearest the library. They'd looked at the timetable and worked it out, so we got to the Library right after it opened in the morning. We were carrying duffle bags with the guns and explosives. When we got close, we put on masks. Then we rushed in and started shooting and shouting at everyone to get down. We shot the guard at the door where you go down to the vault straight away. Two of us went down the stairs with a couple of female hostages and told the guard down there to open up or we'd keep shooting hostages until they did. They did as they were told, so we didn't need to the explosives to get past the gate. The other two of us found the three librarians we needed to open the vault and dragged them downstairs. Same thing: open the vault or we shoot you and the hostages."

"So they opened the vault?"

"Yeah, they opened the vault. Told us it would do us no good, and the police were on their way, but they opened it. It was all fast and smooth. Two of us went into the vault and two of us waited upstairs to control the hostages and cover our exit."

"Then what?"

"Well, the vault wasn't much to look at, just a large room with a plain stone floor and walls lined with metal. In one corner, there were shelves with metal cans on them and a machine with brass dials and knobs, and in another, there was a set of shelves with a few books and other stuff. I remember there was a pair of dice, like for games, just ordinary dice, nothing worth nicking. The strange thing was that they'd built such a large vault and put in so much security when there was hardly anything in it. Only one small set of shelves. We found the papers easy enough because there wasn't anything else that looked like documents on the shelf. So we split them between us and I started to tear my half up and eat it. That's when I saw who's divorce papers they were. They'd said not to look, but I couldn't help myself."

"Who's?"

"The fucking Crown Prince of Scotland and the woman that won the competition to be a princess for two years. Whoever hired us wanted to keep them married."

"Jesus!"

"Yeah, exactly. If I'd have known, I'd have stayed well out of it. Anyway, we tore them up and swallowed them like we were told. It took a while to get the whole lot down. Paper's hard to chew. There was nothing worth nicking on the shelves and we were out of time, so we shot the librarians and ran for it…"

James was shocked. "Why on earth would you shoot the librarians when you were already in the vault?"

"It wasn't my idea. The orders were to kill the three librarians who had the keys and codes to get into the vault. I thought about why they'd tell us to do that after I got locked up. All I came up with was that those three knew the divorce papers were on the shelf in the vault and they'd know we'd destroyed them if they were gone."

"So, did you see anything else in the vault? What did it look like?"

"Like I said, a big room with metal walls and a stone floor. And there were a few things that looked like manhole covers set into the floor. No idea why you'd need manhole covers in a vault. Two lines of five round metal manhole covers. Just like over a drain on a pavement… Oh yeah, and there was one larger cover in a corner. And the whole place smelled strange. Like the smell when they are fixing a road."

"Then what?"

"We ran out the back of the library and into the court building like we were trained to. Went the wrong way a couple of times, it's a maze in there, but in the end, we got out onto Parliament Square. There were no getaway cars waiting for us. Just cops. One of their vans was painted in camouflage colours, like it was army rather than police. It had a weird metal dish on top. They pointed it towards us and suddenly my eyes and skin were burning. I woke up in hospital. They said two of us had died. When we got out of the hospital, they had a trial. There were just three judges, our defence lawyer and the procurer fiscal and it wasn't a normal courtroom. It was much smaller and right in the middle of the building, with no windows. It didn't take long, but to be fair, they had us bang to rights. We were sentenced to life, and the officer made me get in the glass box that took us to the cells. Except it didn't go to the cells. It went to a windowless room which was empty except for a big white chest. The computer told me to get in and when I didn't, it used the pain function on the medical chip they put in us and kept increasing it until I did as I was told. The lid on the chest closed. I heard gas and then the world started spinning and I woke up here. Every couple of weeks, a judge appears on a video screen in my cell and asks if I'm willing to say who hired me. She says if I make a statement, they'll allow euthanasia. But why would I want that when I've got a video game in my cell? I used to live in England. Jail is miles better!"

James tried to do the glitch with the gun again to open the cell door and help the prisoner escape, but now that he was inside a building he couldn't select a weapon. He'd no way of freeing the prisoner and already had the information he wanted, so he quit the game.

"Not finishing a mission, eh?" laughed Milton. "You'll be in Bad Sport forever if you are not careful."

London Calling

It was Marion's last day in Edinburgh before she left for Strasbourg and the team were meeting in the planning room.

"We've found out a fair bit about the security in the library but there must be more to the vault than an almost empty room," said Milton. "There has to be more stuff in that vault than would fit on a single set of shelves. I think there's another level under the one the robbers saw and the stairs down to it are under one of the metal covers they saw."

"Mrs McLinchie told us who constructed the vault: JaS McTear, Banking Engineers from Springburn in Glasgow," said Victoria. "I thought there might be company records, so I tried Googling JaS McTear, but there was nothing."

"Did you try 'James McTear?'" asked James. "People used to write JaS as a contraction for James. There might not be a lot of space on a metal nameplate."

"I'll try again," Victoria got busy on her phone, "OK, that worked! Let's see…"

But a few minutes later, she was no further forward. "They shut down years ago. On Streetview, the factory building is still there, but it's been redeveloped as flats and an artisanal gin distillery. The entire district is gentrified now."

"Knowing the manufacturer's name isn't much help if they are long gone," said James.

"I'm not so sure," said Marion. "If a company invented a clever new safe, they'd be sure to patent it. We need to search for patents assigned to James McTear, Banking Engineers."

Victoria was already on it.

"They've got a bunch of patents on various locks and ways of protecting safes from explosives and fire. They're all online on the European Patent Office website. I'll get the PDFs. Hold on…"

"… there's only one I can't get a PDF for. I just get a note that it is restricted from public access under a national security exemption."

"Well, that's the one we want!"

"OK, I'll hack in." said Victoria, "shouldn't take long."

But a few minutes later, once again, the news was not good.

"I hacked their servers easily enough, but it did no good. They don't have the PDF. It was never digitised. And guess what, the paper copy was moved to…"

"The National Library of Scotland?"

"Exactly. Back to square one."

But Marion had an idea.

"When the vault was constructed in the 1940s, Scotland wasn't independent. We were governed by the English."

"Yeah, so what?"

"So, the Patent Office in London would have a copy of all the patents filed. Nothing Scotland or the EU did would get rid of a paper copy that was held in England. We need to find out where the English have their patent library."

James was busy Googling on his phone.

"It used to be in the British Library near King's Cross Station. But that whole area was flooded just before Scottish Independence - remember, all the sewers in central London became blocked for some reason and the whole place was a metre deep in sewage."

Victoria couldn't help smirking.

"When the Tories leased the land under London to the Hwye'Aye Corporation and the London Underground was built, as part of the deal Hwye'Aye reconstructed London on a concrete plinth above the underground mega-city. The New Georgian Tories didn't want any modern buildings in their capital city, just the old ones. So the new British Library building is gone, as are all their computer and microfilm records, but the paper collection, including the patent library, is back in the Reading Room of the British Museum," James continued.

"If we want to see that patent, it looks like we will need a library card for the British Museum Reading Room and we will need to go to London," said Victoria.

"Why don't we send my husband?" said Marion. "Dealing with the New Georgians sounds like a task for a historian."

— ♦ —

Marion's husband was ecstatic to be offered the chance of an all-expenses paid trip to London to visit the British Museum. He immediately began researching how to get a library card.

"It seems straightforward enough," he told Marion, "obviously they don't have a website and there's no information online, but the New Georgians almost always copy the way things were done in previous centuries. I'll need to travel down to London before applying because the application will need to be done by paper mail with stick on stamps and everything."

"Don't use your real name, David. In a few months, the English might be looking for anyone that has been near this patent." advised Marion.

"Perhaps, while I am in London, I could strengthen my cover story by visiting a few art galleries and the theatre?"

Marion laughed.

"Sure, have fun, David! It's all good as long as you find the patent, photograph it and text the pictures back as soon as you have them."

On his arrival at his hotel in London, David picked up his fountain pen and began to write.

"To the director of the British Museum.

Sir,

I beg to apply for a ticket of admission to the Reading Room of the British Museum. I come from Scotland to study your excellent English whisky and I shall be residing at the McLeod International Hotel and Brothel at King's Cross. I enclose the reference letter of Mr Mitchell, Chief Cashier of the National Bank of Scotland.

Believe me, Sir, to be,

Yours faithfully,

Jock McRichter."

Then he wrote 'Reference from Mr Mitchell' on an envelope and placed a crisp new 50 euro note inside.

Satisfied with his work, he put down the pen. If an application in a false name worked for Lenin in 1902, he could see no reason why it wouldn't work for him.

And indeed, a few days later, a printed form arrived at the McLeod International and was brought to his room.

"The Director of the British Museum begs to inform Mr Jock McRichter that a Reading Ticket will be delivered to Him on presenting this Note to the Clerk in the Reading Room."

'Mr Jock McRichter' and the word 'Him' had been written in by hand, and at the bottom in the same copperplate handwriting:

"Unfortunately, the second half of your recommendation from Mr Mitchell was missing. It should be presented when collecting your ticket."

— ♦ —

David had had a pleasant few days in London, enjoying the theatre, meals with meats and cheeses which were unavailable outside of England and a fresh English strumpet from room service. However, now his Reading Room ticket had been approved, he felt it was prudent to conclude his business and return home. It was only a short walk from his hotel at King's Cross to the British Museum. To his surprise, he saw the Great Court, had been retained after the New Georgian reconstruction of the building, although instead of a modern roof using high-tech materials they had insisted on the same glass and steel technology as in Victorian railway stations so more supporting columns were required. The museum was hosting a special exhibition on "Great English Thinkers of the 21st Century." Red banners with a golden border ran the entire height of the building on either side of the entrance with the names of the eponymous thinkers: "Francois", "Dorries", "Truss" and "Clarkson".

As he entered the Great Court, David's attention was immediately drawn to the bright yellow Lamborghini parked in front of the circular Reading Room. A small plaque next to the car informed him that it had been acquired for the nation with funding from the Department of Culture, since it had once been driven by Clarkson himself. Flanking the car in glass display cases were priceless first edition copies of the works of Clarkson, Dorries, Francois and

Truss from the museum's collection. Each was open to the title page to display the author's signature and dedication. A red velvet rope strung between waist-height golden posts, with a museum security guard in front of each artifact, ensured the crowd kept a respectful distance.

David had been careful to disguise himself in full New Georgian attire purchased from the hotel shop, but as he approached the circular Reading Room in the centre of the court, he noticed a young woman sitting in the Cafe area who was wearing modern clothing: a long black leather coat over a black trouser suit, boots and thin black leather gloves. He was sure he recognised her face, but he couldn't quite place her. The woman noticed he was staring at her. She smiled and beckoned to him to join her and her companion, an athletic looking middle aged man with a military style buzz cut haircut and tailored blue suit.

"Hello, Mr McPherson!" She pulled out a seat. "This gentleman is my colleague. He works for the government."

She noticed David was at a loss and smiled. "You don't remember me? Don't worry, we only met for a few minutes at your wife's leaving party. I'm Justine Cockburn. My husband - actually my wife now - got the Baroness's job on the Supreme Court: Elaine Cockburn."

"Oh, yes, Sheriff Cockburn's wife. I remember. It's my pleasure. But how did you recognise me in London in these clothes?"

"I'm good with faces, I used to be in the police."

Actually, she had been using quite a different sense: one of the advantages of having Labrador DNA inserted in your genome was a supersensitive nose that couldn't be confused by disguises.

Justine turned to the waiter who had come over to take her order.

"Get three coffees ready."

Someone was shouting, David turned and saw an angry looking man in a morning suit was walking rapidly towards them flanked by four museum guards. He was saying something to the nearest guard and pointing at Justine.

David was thinking that it might be prudent to leave, but Justine turned to the waiter again.

"My mistake, four coffees."

She stood up to greet the approaching group.

"Good Morning, Mr Director. Would you care to join us?"

"What do you want? They said something about a court messenger from Scotland? Well, this isn't Scotland!"

"Yes, sir. My name is Justine Cockburn. I am a Messenger at Arms. Unfortunately, your institution has been the subject of proceedings at Edinburgh Sheriff Court and a judgement has been issued against it."

"I don't care about judgements from Scotland. You had best get out, young lady, before I have you thrown out."

Justine took a bulging envelope from the inside pocket of her coat.

"As I said, sir, I am a court messenger from Edinburgh Sheriff Court. I have a copy of the judgement for you."

She held out the envelope. The Director snatched it, walked over to the bin at the entrance to the Cafe and tossed it in.

"Well, now you've delivered it. You can get out."

The four museum guards moved towards Justine.

Justine frowned.

"The Sheriff won't like having his judgment thrown in a bin. He might think that was contempt of court. But, if you'd just turn over everything on his list of stolen items, like I know you're going to, maybe he will overlook it."

"Throw her out!"

The first guard made to grab Justine. She swatted his hand away. A second later, he fell back, clutching his arm which was bleeding heavily. The others kept their distance, unable to see what had caused the wound and thinking discretion might be the better part of valour.

"The Messenger part of my duties is over. If you'll just turn over the items and apologise to the Sheriff, like I know you're going to, there won't be any need for Arms."

More guards were arriving. Some of them were carrying revolvers.

Justine unbuttoned her long leather coat and flicked the material to the side. Under it she was wearing military issue body armour with a 9mm automatic in a holster at her hip. It felt good to be carrying a weapon again. She faced down the guards, her eyes flicking back and forth. As usual, in a combat situation, Justine was channelling her cat side and her tail would also have been twitching from side to side if it hadn't been taped down.

"You have until midnight to inform the court you intend to comply with the order. Now give me the keys to the Lamborghini and I'll be leaving." said Justine, pointing to the supercar from the Clarkson exhibition.

"That car was legitimately donated!"

"Read the last paragraph of the judgement."

The Director retrieved it from the bin and read. "You are also liable to pay the reasonable costs and charges of the Messenger at Arms."

Suddenly, her gun was pointed directly between his eyes.

"Keys!"

The museum director was not accustomed to staring down the barrel of a EU Special Forces issue Glock automatic. He nodded to one of the guards, who fetched the keys from the reception desk.

"Unlock the car, leave the keys in the ignition."

Justine edged towards the car, her right hand keeping her weapon trained on the Director and her left hand in the pocket of her coat.

BLAM!

A dazzling flash and the crash of an explosion came from the far side of the Great Court, behind the Director and his platoon of guards. All eyes turned towards the source of the sound.

All eyes, except Justine's, because she was taking advantage of the distraction caused by the flash-bang to make her escape. Before the guards realised what was happening, the supercar had crashed through the plate glass entrance and was tearing off towards King's Cross and the London Underground.

"You need to leave, sir."

"Sorry?" David turned towards Justine's colleague.

"We need to leave before they lock the place down. I believe you will find it easier to conduct your business tomorrow."

The man didn't wait for a reply. He was already walking quickly towards the nearest exit. It seemed like excellent advice, so

David made himself scarce too.

— ♦ —

The next day, David walked back to the museum to claim his Reading Room Ticket. Despite the forecast from the gentleman from the Scottish Government that it would be easy to do his business today, he'd already decided that if there was any sign of enhanced security he would give up and return to Edinburgh. As he turned the corner of Montague Place, he saw at once that something was wrong. There was no sign of the British Museum: it had simply vanished. Where it had once stood there was now a smooth expanse of concrete, part of the plinth the city had been rebuilt on. The Peelers had placed a cordon around the edge of it and were holding a crowd of curious Londoners back. As David got closer, he saw there was a wooden post set into the concrete with an official notice pinned to it. Eventually, he managed to make his way to the front of the crowd and read it.

"Pursuant to an order granted by Edinburgh Sheriff Court on 17th September 2046, the British Museum has been impounded. Any questions related to this notice should be directed to Justine Cockburn, Messenger at Arms. Block C25, New Paris district, European Union level, London Underground. Business Hours: 9am to 5pm."

David returned to King's Cross and used the entrance to the London Underground in the station concourse. After scanning his iris to confirm his identity as an EU citizen, he was able to take the escalator down to the Gare du Nord in New Paris. He opened the map on his phone and searched for block C25 of New Paris. Surprisingly, it was within easy walking distance of the Gare du Nord.

He made his way through the bustling New Parisian streets. The pavement cafes and bistros were packed with people enjoying a pleasant lunch and a glass of wine. The restaurants of New Paris were popular lunch destinations for residents of many areas of the city. The roof of the underground city above New Paris was covered in digital displays to simulate the sky, and the current setting was a sunny summer day. All except the roof above block C25 which had no displays, just naked grey concrete. The second unusual thing about block C25 was the British Museum. From a distance it appeared to be floating in midair between the top of the four story high Parisian tenements and the grey concrete roof. As he got closer, the thick concrete plinth under the museum, the scaffolding of beams which supported it and the array of heavy-duty electric jacks which had lowered it down, came into view.

The site office was on the first floor of one of the Parisian tenements above a bar. Justine was sitting at her desk, working on the computer. She looked up and smiled as David came in.

"You've impounded the British Museum!" said David, flabbergasted.

"The Sheriff ordered it to be impounded, I'm just enforcing his judgement."

"How on earth did you do it?"

"Construction Robotics, the company who built the London Underground carried out the work under contract. It was an expensive project, but there are a lot of valuable artifacts to be recovered. They used a laser cutting tool to cut through the plinth all the way around the museum in the middle of the night, lowered it down gently on electric jacks and then a concrete printing robot reconstructed the plinth."

"But how does an Edinburgh Sheriff's Officer manage to get a case like this?"

"It started because the First Minister was absolutely livid at the English raid on the National Library of Scotland. She instructed Tourism Scotland to raise an action in Edinburgh Sheriff Court for the return of the Lewis Chessmen to provide legal justification for a quid-pro-quo commando raid on the British Museum. For some reason, none of the established Sheriff's Officer companies wanted to take part in a military raid on England, so I got the business."

"But you took the entire building, not just a chess set!" David spluttered.

"To be honest, it all got a bit out of hand after the case was filed. Nobody had considered just how much stuff the English stole from other countries and put in the British Museum when they had their empire. The Greek and Egyptian governments asked to join Tourism Scotland as plaintiffs and the Sheriff certified the case against the British Museum as a class action. After that, the flood gates opened. There are now twenty-five nation state plaintiffs and so many items to recover that the only practical solution was to impound the whole building. Fortunately, I've got an extremely competent personal assistant who worked out all the details. But what brings you here? Do you have business at the museum?"

"I was hoping to use the Reading Room. There are some historic documents I need to research. I wonder if you could let me in?"

"I'd like to help but I'm here to enforce a court order: unless the property is on the list of stolen items, I must act on behalf of the museum and apply their rules for accessing the collection."

David took the letter from his pocket.

"I have a letter from the museum saying I can collect a Reading Room Ticket." He handed it over.

Justine examined it carefully.

"Well, this seems straightforward enough. I see that you have applied with a false name, but if they didn't care to check your identity before issuing the document, I have no responsibility to do so. You just have to give me the second half of the reference as they requested, then you can go on in, collect your ticket and look for your documents."

David took out a fifty euro note.

Justine smiled, "Ah, I see, 'a reference from Mr Mitchell.' I'll add this to their assets, if there is anything left after the creditor's claims and the costs of enforcing the judgement are deducted it will be passed on to them."

She looked up at the camera in the corner of the room.

"Computer. Add David McPherson, to the access list for the Reading Room."

"Mr David McPherson, added to access list."

"That's it David. Just scan your iris at the barrier to get into the building."

It took a few hours to locate the patent documents since there were no museum staff to help, but before the end of the day, he had photographed the patent and e-mailed the photos to Marion.

— ♦ —

James helped Victoria carry the shiny silver model of the vault she had 3D printed through to the planning room. It took pride of place on the table near the whiteboards.

"Well, the good news is that now we know how this vault works," she said, "the bad news is it is nothing like any other vault in the world and there is no way to defeat the mechanism. The slightly better news is we don't need to defeat the mechanism."

"Just tell us how it works," put in Milton, "I'm not exactly an amateur when it comes to robbing banks."

Victoria smiled.

"The safe mechanism in the vault provides a time delay. Each item stored in the safe is only accessible one day per year. Nobody, not even the library staff, can access it on any other day. Items go into the safe and they come out again exactly one year later. At that point, the librarians decide whether to put them back into the safe for another year or take them out to the main library. If we want to steal the TDA source code, we can only do it on the day it is accessible."

"Nonsense! We could use explosives or a laser drill on the lock."

"There is no lock. The mechanism in this vault is far simpler than that."

Milton started to mutter something about kidnapping the Chief Librarian's family.

"That will not work either since the librarians cannot control the mechanism. It would be faster if you would let me explain what the mechanism is."

Milton nodded sulkily.

"The inventor of the safe was a Glasgow safe maker and, as an undergraduate, he'd been shown Lord Kelvin's pitch glacier experiment in the Hunterian Museum. The experiment shows that pitch, while appearing solid, for example cracking into pieces if you hit it with a hammer, also has some of the properties of a liquid, only it moves at a very slow pace. The pitch glacier has moved around a metre in 150 years."

"So what has this got to do with a safe?"

"The safe described in the patent is a fifty-metre shaft cut through solid rock which is filled with a pitch or tar-like substance, presumably somewhat softer than that used in Kelvin's experiment. A valuable object to be preserved is loaded into a specially designed metal container. Lead shot is added to control the weight of the container and it is sealed. Then it is simply placed in the shaft. The properties of the pitch and the density of the container are calculated so it takes exactly one year to fall from the top to the bottom of the shaft. From the robber's description of what he saw in the vault, I would surmise that as an additional measure there are ten such shafts. He also mentioned there was a pair of dice on one of the shelves at the top of the vault. My guess is they are choosing a shaft at random for each item to be stored and keep no record of which shaft was used. All they need to do is check the bottom of each shaft every day to see if any capsules have arrived."

"So to fish the capsule with the TDA source code out before it gets to the bottom, you would need to dig through potentially tens of meters of almost solid pitch and you wouldn't even know which shaft to start digging in?"

"That is the idea. Retrieving a capsule before it comes out by itself would require far more time than a robber would ever have in the vault."

"We could melt the pitch," suggested Milton, "although the energy required would be considerable."

"If we did that, it would be obvious the vault had been robbed," said Marion. She was already in Strasbourg but had called into the meeting. Victoria had supplied her with a burner phone with an app which provided strong encryption."I need to smuggle a document into the vault. If they know the vault has been tampered with, the provenance of anything that comes out of the vault will be questioned."

"There is an easier way," said Victoria. "We can find out the day the TDA source code was added to the vault. It was the day before the Political Correctness Enforcement Act was signed by the King, and that is a matter of record. We need to rob the vault on the anniversary of that day."

James typed a search into the computer.

"The Political Correctness Act became law on January 16. Anthony told me the TDA Source code was sent to the National Library of Scotland the day before the King signed the law, so that would be January 15. We have nearly three months to wait."

"What about leap years and so on? The time to fall through the shaft is a physical phenomenon, it won't be an exact calendar year."

"That's a good point, the robber said the papers were on a shelf at the top of the vault, maybe they use that to store things for an extra day so they can align the physical delay with the calendar year for leap years."

"The details of how they do it don't matter. We know they manage the vault so they can extract items on the calendar anniversary of the day they went in. From what James was told by the robber in the game world, there are no further locks once you are inside the vault. If we get into it on the anniversary of the day that TDA 6 was stored in the vault and we look at the bottom of the shafts and in the working area at the top, we will find it."

"The royal marriage was on December 10 the year before last, that's the date when the post-dated divorce papers would have been filed and December 10 last year was when the attempted robbery happened," said Marion, "so I need to put the new documents in the vault on December 10th."

"Why not put the documents in when we get the TDA code in January but put some extra weight in the capsule so it falls faster?" asked James.

"That would only work if there was nothing else in the tube. Otherwise, it may catch up with and bang into some other capsule halfway and throw off our calculations about the weight," said Milton.

"So we need to rob this vault twice, December 10, to restore the divorce papers and January 15 to get the TDA 6 source code," said Victoria.

There was silence.

After a minute, Milton started to say something, but James cut him short.

"Yeah, we know, we can't go the same way twice. It's too soon. We will need to use a different approach."

The Heist

They'd just locked up for the night and James was in the manager's office of the arcade with Claire. Claire had gradually become a permanent fixture in the arcade. It wasn't totally clear whether she was a regular customer with privileges to take free coffee and cake or an unpaid staff member. Claire liked to wear tinted shades and a bobble hat like the NPC bartender from the arcade in the game when she worked behind the bar, but she'd just changed into the 'slutty' variant of the Brothel uniform. Thanks to the sentence she'd taken on to allow Marion to go to Strasbourg, she had to do two hours in the red-light windows after work. As usual, Milton was on the videoconferencing screen, standing beside the whiteboards in his arcade.

"If we can't get in through the library itself because of all the new security, the new tram tunnel is the closest thing to the vault," said Milton, "We are going to have to get into that tunnel and have a look about, and the best way will be through the tram stop they are building under the courts. There's nobody in the court buildings in the middle of the night. Anyone that needs to be locked up is moved to the Brothel after the courts shut. Even the escorts and the red-light windows are shut at midnight. There's probably nothing watching the whole complex of buildings except the image processing computers hooked up to the CCTV cameras and I've got control of them."

"We can't go tonight. Marion is in Strasbourg with her new husband, and Victoria needs to get a babysitter to come out after school hours," said James.

"We don't need them. It only takes one person to have a quick look. The Inmate Transport System goes straight past the new tram stop, I've hacked their system and I can send you right to it from the DIshonesty Box in the arcade, and there'll only be a plywood hoarding to get through."

"OK, I'll go," said James reluctantly. "Let's do it in the middle of the night when there's nobody around."

But Claire had another idea.

"Why don't we do it now? The courts are already shut, but the brothel areas are still open for business. I need to go to the red-light windows for my sentence, anyway. If I get caught, all I need to say is the pod stopped, but the door was open, so I thought I could just walk the rest of the way."

"If you are sure," James couldn't quite hide his relief.

"It's not a big deal. Give me a minute to get in the pod."

"When you're ready, call us from the pod. You will need your hands to be free and it will be noisy near the tunnel, so use your headphones," said Milton.

When Claire called, James put her on speaker.

"OK - I'm ready. I'm in the pod."

Milton locked the door of the pod and sent it on its way. It lowered slowly through the floor of the arcade, past empty court offices on the two floors below, and into the basement. The pod was pushed off the hoist which moved it vertically within the building onto a conveyor and started its journey westwards through a narrow tunnel under the court buildings. Other conveyor belts split off to the side at regular intervals, but the system kept Claire's pod moving straight ahead. There was a small light in the pod, but the passage was pitch-black, and she soon had no idea where she was in relation to the above-ground buildings. She started counting and when she got to a hundred, the pod suddenly shunted to the right. She was on a different conveyor belt. Shortly after that, it stopped. The conveyor system was noisy, but there was a much louder noise here. It took her a second to realise it was the tunnel boring machine.

"Milton, I've stopped, but it's totally dark. They turn all the lights out when the buildings close."

"Sorry, I don't have control of the lights. Didn't think to hack that system. Can you use the light on your phone?"

Claire switched on the light from her phone. Her transport pod had stopped opposite a dark blue plywood hoarding which blocked off access to the construction site.

There was a click as Milton unlocked the transparent cell. She pushed the door open and looked around. The system the Brothel used to move its inmate transport pods around had been designed for warehouses, and the conveyor was a few feet above the ground. Climbing down was out of the question in a Brothel issue miniskirt and four-inch heels.

"Milton, I'm not going to be able to climb out in these heels and I need to stay clean. The whole place is coated in dust from the construction. I can take some video with my phone."

"Is there anybody about? Is it safe?"

"There's nobody anywhere near here."

There was a loud rumbling noise from the tram tunnel, which took some time to pass.

"Something went past in the tram tunnel, something big."

"It will be the transporter with the tailings dug out by the boring machine."

James was feeling more courageous after seeing the video from Claire's phone.

"Claire, you've done all you can in those clothes. Milton, bring a booth for me. I'll get the coveralls and toolbox from the cleaning cupboard and take over."

Five minutes later, James was standing next to the wooden hoarding. His head torch gave a much better view than the light on Claire's phone and he could see the builders had put a door in the hoarding and secured it with a padlock. There was a large warning sign next to the door: "WARNING. FULLY AUTOMATED CONSTRUCTION SITE. DO NOT ENTER WHILE EQUIPMENT IS ACTIVE. DANGER OF DEATH." and next to it another one, just in case you hadn't got the message "HAZARDOUS AREA, NO ENTRY. HEAVY EQUIPMENT. LIVE ELECTRIC CABLES. UNSAFE NOISE LEVELS. UNSAFE DUST LEVELS." The company apparently considered their signs were so terrifying there was no need for further precautions against trespassing. There were only four wood screws fixing the metal plate the padlock went through to the door frame and it was quick work to take them out. He took some duct tape from the toolbox and stuck the screws to the hoarding to make sure they didn't roll away and get lost. Then he stepped out into the new tram stop.

Even though the boring machine was some distance further along the tunnel, the noise was intense and James had to pull his T-shirt over his mouth against the dust. He was standing on a raised concrete platform beside the tram track. At first he was surprised to see the track was already installed, but then he realised the tunnelling machines were laying it as they went because they moved along it themselves. He took out his phone to video the scene for Milton. Suddenly, the track started to hum and almost immediately, the empty tailings transporter rumbled past on its way back to the face of the excavation. Shortly behind the transporter, two much smaller construction robots followed up the track. One had a cutter, and the other had a tank full of concrete and a robotic arm with a nozzle to pump it out.

"Did you see that, Milton?"

"Yeah, it's not surprising they've got robots for cutting and laying concrete. The boring machine will line the tunnel with pre-cast concrete sections as it moves forward, but they'll need to cut refuge spaces every so often so staff can get out the way of trams and to provide spaces for equipment."

"The concrete robot has stopped, it seems to be working on extending the end of this platform. It's like a 3D printer except with concrete."

"Maybe we can make use of those robots. We should be able to hack in and get control of them. I guess when it is time for the tailings transport to come back, we will see those two return first, since there's only one track."

"I was thinking about that. How come there aren't two tracks? Usually, the trams have one for each direction."

"It's costing a fortune to bore through the volcanic rock. They probably thought they could live with just one tunnel for a few hundred metres and fix the schedule so the trams in each direction can share it."

"Knowing the council, I bet they end up building the second one in a few years and it costs far more than it would if they just did them both now!" said James. "Have you seen everything you need? I can't stay down here for long, there's too much dust."

"It's OK. You can go back to the transport pod. The only thing I still need is for you to listen for when the tailings transport comes back again, so we know how long we would have to explore the tunnel between its runs."

When he got back to the arcade, James washed up and went back to the planning room to look at their map.

"Getting into the tram tunnel is definitely easier than getting into the library, but what good is it when the path of the tunnel never gets closer than fifty metres from the vault," said James. "How on earth are we going to get through all that rock, never mind do it without anyone noticing?"

"Who says the tunneling machine is going to follow the planned route?" said Milton with a chuckle. "The next step is to find out how they guide that machine."

— ♦ —

Once again, the job of exploring the tunnel fell to James and Claire, but this time, they were much better prepared. Although she was dodging most of the dangerous work, Victoria was making herself useful by sourcing equipment. She'd got them industrial ear defenders, fancy noise cancelling in-ear bluetooth headsets to wear under them as a second line of defence, helmets, work boots with a steel toe cap, coveralls with a hood, and full-face masks with an air filter and eye protection. As an extra precaution, in case they were spotted on CCTV, she'd copied the logo of the construction company and put it on the back of the coveralls. They looked like a cross between SWAT and a biohazard cleanup team.

Milton decided to give them a briefing before they went in.

"The public information on the tunnelling company's website suggests they are using a laser based system to dead-reckon the position of the boring machine underground. It's too deep for them to be able to use GPS. We also know from hacking the Council's CCTV archive that every two weeks, a van from the Scottish distributor of the market leading laser theodolite enters the construction site on Chambers Street. The vibration data from the council seismometers shows there is no vibration on those mornings, which means the tunnelling is halted. The obvious conclusion is they are setting up a laser theodolite to guide the machine for the next segment of the tunnel."

"We know all this, Milton. Let's go, already! It's hot in these suits."

"Well, if you don't want the briefing, on you go without it, then!" said Milton grumpily, "just don't blame me if things go horribly wrong."

James and Claire picked up the metal cases with their equipment and went to the Dishonesty Box to be transported. When they got out, they unscrewed the metal plate securing the door in the construction site hoarding and were relieved to discover that conditions on the tram platform were much more bearable with the masks and ear defenders.

"OK, now we wait for the tailings transporter. If it's on the same schedule, it should be here any…"

With no warning, the transporter burst out from the tunnel on their right.

"Milton, these ear defenders and headsets work so well we can't hear it coming! This is crazy dangerous!"

"It's just this one time. Once you place the microphones, I'll know what's moving in the tunnel and I'll be able to give you a warning. It's a pity we can't use cameras but Victoria was right, they'd get covered in dust too quickly and they're bigger and harder to conceal. That transporter was going south to be unloaded. James, you have ten minutes to run north along the tunnel before you need to get in a refuge. Claire, you are going south. You don't have as much time, so stop at the first refuge. Get on the phone and warn James as soon as you see or hear the transport returning. The clock is ticking, go!"

Claire jumped onto the tracks and started to run south, James began to run north.

James had got about 50 metres into the tunnel when he heard Claire scream. He stopped and started to run back.

"Claire, what is it? What's happened?"

"Forget it! Keep going. I'll tell you when we are safe!"

Based on what they'd seen in other parts of the tram network they were expecting that there'd be refuges every fifty or a hundred metres, but it seemed to Claire that she'd been running a lot further than that and she hadn't found one. Maybe the equipment was slowing her down. She couldn't get what she'd just seen out of her head or the fact that she was running towards the transporter. Her safety margin was getting smaller with every step and she'd be crushed for sure if she didn't reach a refuge soon. She'd come so far that turning back and trying to get to the platform was almost certainly even more dangerous than going forward. She was getting out of breath. The dust filter made it hard to get enough oxygen to run. But she could see the first refuge in the light of her head torch now. She bruised her leg in the desperate scramble to get off the track and out of the path of the transporter, which she was sure would be returning any moment. Finally safe, she collapsed, trying to recover her breath and calm herself.

She'd been in the refuge for about a minute when the transporter burst out of the darkness to her left.

"James! It just went past me. Get off the tracks and in a refuge fast!"

"I'm safe!" James reported, gasping for breath. "I'm in the second refuge from the tram platform heading north. I'm sure they are over a hundred meters apart!"

Claire could hear the rumble of the transporter over her headset, it must have reached James. That thing was fast!

"It just passed me," said James. "Why did you scream before?"

"There was a huge bloodstain. Something was scraped along the tunnel wall and torn apart. Maybe it was a fox, there was fur."

"That's not good," said James. "A fox is a lot smaller than a person. If it hits something that size and we aren't in a refuge when it goes past, we have had it. Lying flat on the ground or pushing ourselves against the wall of the tunnel isn't going to be enough."

"You need to focus," said Milton. "Forget the dead fox, you have to hide one of your microphones near where you are now. Then go forward to the next refuge. We have one hour before the transporter returns. Claire, you should have enough time to put microphones in the refuge you are in and the next one and get back to the tram platform."

Claire found a cement joint between two concrete sections near the refuge and opened her rucksack to get the microphone and tools she'd brought. She made a hole with a screwdriver, pushed in the microphone, and concealed it with a thin layer of filler.

"Milton, the first microphone is in place. Just next to the first refuge after the tram platform."

"OK, I'm getting a signal. It's good. Go on to the next refuge!"

After seeing what happened to the fox, Claire didn't have to be told about the need to hurry. She wanted to get out of the tunnel as fast as possible. She ran south down the tunnel, but instead of another refuge, she saw a glimmer of light.

"Milton, there are no more refuges on this side. I can see light ahead. I think it's the construction site in Chambers Street."

"OK. If you ran seventy five or a hundred metres to the first refuge, you could well be more than halfway to the construction site. Don't get too close, maybe go a little further and then look for somewhere to place your second microphone. The further up the tunnel we get it, the more warning we will have of the transporter returning. Once you are done, go back to the tram platform and wait for James."

"The first microphone is done and I'm almost at the next refuge Milton," said James, "the tunneling machine just started up again and it's noisy as hell here even with ear protectors."

"OK, let me check. Yeah, I'm getting data from your first microphone. We are at twenty minutes. Keep going."

"Second refuge, now!" The noise from the boring machine was so loud James needed to shout.

"OK, place your microphone. Do you think you can stay there until the tailings transporter makes another trip?"

"Yeah, maybe. There's a lot of grit in the air and it is noisy, but with the mask and ear defenders it's possible."

"Can you see how much further up the tunnel it is from where you are to the boring machine?"

"No. The tunnel is full of dust and there are small stones flying about. It is so loud here I think it must be close, but all I can see in my head torch beam is dust. Once I place the microphone, I'm going to get as far back into the refuge as I can."

"OK, just sit tight."

"That's it done."

"It's working, the audio data is off the scale!"

There were still ten minutes before the transporter would return.

"Milton, it's getting harder to breathe."

"The filter on your mask might be getting blocked up with dust, but it is far too late for you to run back to the platform. You are going to have to hold out. As soon as they stop boring the dust level will fall."

James felt claustrophobic. Now he'd been told the filter might be blocked, it felt like he was suffocating. He knew this was exactly the wrong time to have a panic attack, but that didn't stop it from happening.

Fortunately for James, this was 2046: the MedChip within his abdomen noted that he was hyperventilating and had raised levels of stress hormones and the software dispensed a small dose of his anxiety medication.

"James, are you OK?" asked Claire.

"Yeah, I think so. I feel better now. I'm definitely not getting as much air as before, but it is enough."

The wall of sound around him suddenly ceased.

"The tunneling machine has stopped!"

"I know. The noise has stopped on the microphone you planted."

"There's something else happening. I heard a 'clunk' noise. I think the tailings transport has uncoupled itself ready to make a run back to Chambers Street."

"How is the dust level?"

"Still pretty bad, but less than before."

"OK, you need to wait for the tailings transporter to pass you and then you need to walk up the tunnel towards the boring machine."

"You're kidding! There are probably no more refuges between me and the tunneling machine. When that thing comes back, I'll have nowhere to go."

"You need to get back to your refuge before it comes back. You've got maybe ten minutes. The time when the transporter is not attached, and the boring has stopped, is their opportunity to use a laser to check the alignment. There is less dust and the back of the boring machine is not hidden behind the transporter."

"Here it comes!"

"You only have ten minutes. Don't mess about!"

As soon as the transporter passed, James climbed down from the refuge onto the tram track and ran north. The dust was clearing and almost immediately he could pick out something large directly in front of him.

"I think I can see the boring machine now! It was very close."

James became aware of a green laser beam cutting through the dusty air from somewhere behind him and focussed on a camera on the back of the boring machine.

"I can see a green laser. It came on after the dust cleared a bit."

"OK, find where it is coming from."

"I'm looking. The source is back down the tunnel a bit. I must have run straight past it."

He walked back down the track towards the laser.

"Found it! There's a pit in between the tracks with a metal cover over it and it has popped up out of that. The cover must have been shut before and I ran straight over it."

"Hiding it away while the boring is happening will keep it cleaner, and it means it doesn't block the tracks. What does it look like?"

"It looks just like the one on the manufacturer's website. It's a standard theodolite, mounted on a fancy platform so it can be retracted and hidden away under the track level."

"OK, moment of truth. The lens on the theodolite should unlock after a quarter turn. Get the lens Victoria made for us ready and swap them over as fast as you can. We don't want dust getting in. Oh, and try not to look into the laser. We should really have got you special goggles for this bit!"

"So basically, do this fiddly job without looking?"

"Yes, and once you do it, run like hell to get back to the refuge before the transporter comes back and flattens you."

James' MedChip decided to give him more medication. So at least he wasn't terrified. On the other hand, being artificially calm wasn't going to help him run any faster.

The lens came off unexpectedly easily and James fumbled and dropped it. Thankfully, the new lens went on equally easily and clicked reassuringly into place after a quarter turn. There was no time to do anything except grab the old one and run for the refuge. As he bent down to pick it up, the green laser flicked off, and the assembly started to descend back into its pit.

"Run! The transporter just left the Chambers Street end. It's coming back!" shouted Milton.

James ran for his life. He was almost at the refuge, but he could already see the light on the front of the transporter approaching. For a second he thought he would be smeared along the tunnel wall like the fox, but miraculously the light didn't seem to be getting closer.

"I'm OK, safe in the refuge. It needs to slow right down before it docks with the boring machine, and that gave me a few more seconds."

Claire breathed a sigh of relief.

The deafening noise started up again. That meant the tailings transporter was docked in place to catch the debris.

"Were there any other robots coming down the tunnel after the transporter?" James asked.

"I didn't hear anything," said Milton.

"I've not seen anything pass the tram platform," said Claire.

"OK, I'm coming back."

James walked back down the tunnel to the tram platform. Even walking, he had to pause and catch his breath every few minutes because the filter in his mask was so choked with dust.

When they arrived back at the arcade, they packed all their dusty gear away in bin bags and spend ten minutes with a vacuum to get the inmate transport pod clean again before washing up and going to the planning room.

"I dropped the lens," James confessed, "the one that was on before. I'm pretty sure it will be broken. The new one is on properly though."

"If I am right about how they do things it won't matter," said Milton, "As long as we don't take the laser more than a little off true with our lens and as long as the theodolite engineer just moves it from the previous pit forward to the new pit every two weeks and then sets the new alignment, we should be fine. We'd only have a problem if they took the theodolite with our lens on it back to their office to clean or recalibrate. I'll keep an eye on their e-mail so we will know if they spot something is wrong."

"So we need to do this again in two weeks?"

"We only need to swap the lens when we need a different skew on the laser from the previous section. We'll definitely need to do it a few times. The most critical one will be just before the tunneling machine gets closest to the vault. Once it is past the vault and we have it back on its planned course, we just put on a lens with no skew and we are done."

"Why don't we just change the angle on the platform to set course, same as the engineer, instead of messing about with new lenses?" asked James.

"Because the engineer is bound to have the correct angles written down, and he's going to notice if they are wrong," said Milton, "and before you ask, we can't just change it back before he comes. As soon as we changed it back, the laser wouldn't be aimed at the camera on the back of the boring machine. The boring machine would notice it was off course."

— ♦ —

Six weeks later, the preparatory work was finished. Claire and James had been in the tunnel three more times to replace the lens on the laser theodolite. The resulting course changes had brought the tunneling machine to within three metres of the vault and then returned it to its original course. Victoria had also hacked in to the tunneling company's servers and instructed the smaller construction robots to make a refuge opening in the tunnel lining directly opposite the vault and dig back as far as the arm on the cutting robot could reach from its position on the tram track. Now was the moment of truth.

James took their newly purchased drill out of his duffel bag and fitted the longest and thinnest bit. Victoria had said according to her calculations only fifteen centimetres of rock remained before the vault, but then she started talking about 'tolerances' and finally mentioned a 'margin of error' of ten centimetres. So there was somewhere between five and twenty-five centimetres of rock to drill through. Tentatively, he pushed the drill forward, alert for any change that might indicate he was about to break through earlier than expected. The bit sunk deeper and deeper into the rock. After five centimetres, James changed to the largest of the bits and drilled out a wider hole. Then he started again with the thin bit. Soon, there was a distinct change in tone. They'd touched the lining of the vault. He stopped immediately and handed over to Claire, relieved that he'd completed his task without mishap. They'd agreed that Claire would do the delicate final part. Slowly and carefully, she chipped away at the remaining material with the smallest drill bit until they could see the material lining the inside of the vault.

"It's a tile," said Claire. "we should go sideways and try to find the gap between two tiles. It will be less noticeable to break through there."

"Yeah, good idea. The grout between tiles will be softer and less brittle than the tiles themselves."

They worked slowly, drilling away rock until finally they came to the gap between two tiles.

"OK, here goes!"

Claire picked a tiny hole in the grout between the tiles with a screwdriver, while James held the nozzle of a handheld vacuum cleaner as close as possible to suck up loose material. They didn't want any debris falling into the vault.

"OK, now for the fibre-optic camera."

They attached the body of the camera to the rock next to the hole they'd created and extended the thin fibre optic cable through the hole. Then they made a second small hole for a microphone. Once the camera and microphone were in place, they filled in the hole they'd drilled with polystyrene foam to dampen the sound from the tunnel.

"Can't see a thing!" said Milton when they switched on the camera. "The picture is dark."

"Well, of course it is. There's not going to be any light in a vault in the middle of the night. We're going to have to wait until the librarians open the vault in the morning."

The next morning they huddled around the screen in the arcade office bright and early, waiting for the librarians to show up in the vault. Sure enough, at eight am sharp, they heard metallic clanging noises in the distance and then the picture became slightly less dark. Soon they could make out a dim light swaying from side to side.

"They're coming down the stairs!"

Eventually, two forms emerged. Both were carrying lanterns which they hung on hooks suspended on cables from the ceiling.

"Those are pretty bright lanterns. I thought they weren't allowed anything electrical in the vault?"

"I think they are gas lanterns, not the oil ones in old movies."

They could see the base of the vault properly now. It was a cramped and low tunnel which encircled a solid column of rock several meters wide. The tiles had probably once been glossy, like those in an old tenement or Victorian swimming baths, dark green near the ground, switching to white at about shoulder height. They were now dirty and stained. The floor had rougher, matt tiles, with a natural stone finish. The tar tubes were drilled through the rock column in a two by five array with more than a metre of of solid rock between neighbouring tubes. The tunnel was wider near the metal staircase which led up to the top of the vault and the library had used the extra space for a workbench.

Each of the tar tubes had a mechanism at its base, the metal was jet black with age and exposure to the tar. As they watched, a librarian donned work gloves and then went round them in turn. When he got to the tube nearest their camera, they could see he was lighting a gas burner.

"He's softening the tar," whispered Milton.

"We know, and there's no need to whisper. They can't hear us!" said Claire.

After the gas had been running for a few minutes, the librarian picked up a long, thin metal rod with a wooden handle and went to the first of the tar pits. He opened a small flap near the bottom of the column and pushed the rod in, moving it to and fro, probing the tar.

"Nothing in number one tube," he said, "turning the gas off."

The second librarian had also collected a metal rod and was performing the same operation on the second tube.

"Number two is empty!"

"I keep saying we should just write down when we put something in a tube and which one we used so we know where it is going to come out. It would save so much time!"

"And I keep telling you, if a record like that fell into the wrong hands, it would tell a robber where to start searching and defeat the purpose of having ten columns. We throw dice to decide which one to use and we don't write anything down. Once I retire and you are Chief Librarian, you can make the rules, but as long as I'm in charge, we will follow the manufacturer's instructions!"

"Well, you changed the security upstairs after the attempted robbery. The locks on the hatches and the door to get down here aren't original features. There's nothing wrong with learning from experience. And my experience is that it stinks of tar down here and checking all ten tubes every day is a pain in the arse."

"Pain in the arse or not, the fact is that the system worked. The armed robbers got into the vault, but they didn't manage to steal anything."

"Hold on, there's one here. Tube four."

The librarian put a chalk cross on the tube and moved on to the next.

After a while, it seemed like they'd checked everything.

"Just one today, then. Let's give it another minute to soften up."

"C'mon, we could use a workout!"

They started to turn a large wheel on the front of the stove-like arrangement at the bottom of the tar tube. It looked like hard work at first, but then it went faster. As they turned, a steel drawer slowly moved out from the base of the apparatus, just above the gas burner. When it was out, one of the librarians went over to the workbench and returned with a pair of tongs. With some difficulty, he pulled a container out of the sticky tar in the steel drawer. His colleague immediately began spinning the wheel in the opposite direction to close the drawer again.

The four conspirators, Milton, Claire, Victoria and James, were glued to the monitor. Marion was at work in Strasbourg and had been unwilling to take a call about a robbery from her office in the European Court. She was now only in Edinburgh when she had to attend a meeting of one of the committees which Justice Cockburn had not yet qualified to take over.

As they watched, the capsule retrieved from the tar pit was cleaned with solvent and wiped off, then placed in a clamp on the workbench. The librarian tightened thumb-wheels at several points around the circumference of the clamp to lock it in place. Then, using a tool with a cap that fitted over the top of the capsule and a long handle for leverage, he twisted the capsule open. It took a hard pull to get the lid moving, but he could soon put the tool to one side and unscrew the rest of the way by hand.

"That's a torque wrench," said Milton. "You can see the dial on the shaft. There must be a specified torque they want the lid tightened to."

One of the librarians swapped his heavy work gloves for white cotton gloves before taking a black felt bag out of the opened capsule. They inspected a label attached to the drawstring.

"Can we move the camera?" asked Milton, "we need a close-up of the bag and the label on it."

"No, I bought a simple fibre optic camera," said Victoria, "the supplier has an endoscopic one you can move about, and one with a second fibre for a light source but they are thicker and I thought they'd be more likely to be spotted."

"October 15, 2050. This one's got a few more years. The capsule looks OK to me. What do you think?" asked the first librarian.

"Yeah, it opened up nice and smoothly. There's no leakage. It's fine for another trip."

"Right, let's stick whatever this is back in. Just check we've turned off all the gas while I finish up."

The librarians put a little oil on the thread, then screwed the capsule shut, finally tightening it with the torque wrench. Then they removed it from the clamp on the workbench, retrieved their lanterns and went upstairs. A door clanged shut, and the vault was completely dark again. A few moments later there was another clang from above, a flat noise like something hitting damp earth and then a second clang. Finally, a heavy clunk.

James rewound and replayed the audio.

"What do you think?"

"I think the first noise was the librarians opening and closing the door at the top of the steps, then we heard them open the cover on one of the pits, then the capsule hitting the tar, then the cover being closed and finally the heavy vault door closing behind them," said Victoria.

"I agree."

"The walls look really filthy, especially near the ground," said Claire.

"It will be fumes and droplets from the tar. They've been at the bottom of a tar pit for more than a hundred years. They won't trust a regular cleaner to come down here and the chief librarian and his deputy aren't going to scrub tar off tiles themselves," said Victoria. "The dirt is good for us, it will make it easier to conceal the cut when we make our entrance."

"If we cut the grout between the tiles, not the tiles themselves, it will be easier to patch up behind us," said James, "The best thing would be to make the smallest possible passage we can wriggle through, low down to the floor on the dark green tiles. If we get the tiles off intact we can mount them on a piece of plywood and make a panel we can take in and out."

"Seems straightforward enough," said Victoria. "I'll buy a small robot to do the tiling and woodworking and drill out the material behind the tiles. I can calculate the instructions for the robot if you can get me photos of the space in the tunnel where it will be working."

"Just remember, the robot will need to break down into parts which are small and light enough for us to carry up the tunnel! And we should get some spare battery packs so it can work longer because there's nowhere to charge it in there," said Claire.

"How's the money holding up?" asked Milton.

"There's still about 10k left from the money we got to fund the heist," said James. "Victoria, you've been buying a lot of stuff. We must owe you quite a bit. You need to ask!"

"Oh, don't worry. The least I can do is contribute a little money to make up for not being able to get out at night and help in the tunnel. Which reminds me, it's nearly time to collect my son from school."

She stood up and gave everyone a quick wave before grabbing her coat.

"There's more to that one than we know." said Milton. "She's got money to buy robots without a thought and to send a kid to Farnon's and she looks exactly like the game character who started this off."

"She told me she got pregnant by a customer when she was working for the Brothel. The Brothel made a mistake and disabled her contraception when they reprogrammed her MedChip with sex worker settings, part of the compensation was she got a licence to keep the child and they paid for school," said Claire.

"Remember the first time she was here, and you told me to hire her," said James. "Well, I can tell you, she's expensive. She could be making good money."

"Maybe." said Milton, "I don't think she's a cop, but I don't trust her. I don't trust her even more than I don't trust the rest of you."

"That's OK Milton," Claire replied with a grin, "we don't trust you either."

— ♦ —

There were only a few days left before the divorce papers had to go back in the vault. James and Claire were in the tunnel every night, lugging equipment and material back and forth from the tram station to the refuge where they had dug their access to the vault. They never saw anyone else and the tailings collector was less of a threat now that they had microphones in place and knew its schedule. The small construction robots Victoria had bought were fast and accurate, but the tough igneous rock was hard on both drill bits and batteries.

They had experimented in the arcade and confirmed that Claire and Victoria could both squeeze through a hole five tiles high and four across. The tiles were rectangular, so despite having more tiles in the vertical dimension, the cutout shape was longer than it was high. The final piece of the puzzle fell into place when the forged divorce papers to be placed in the vault were delivered to a dead drop in Holyrood Park. They were ready.

For the first time, Victoria arranged for Justine to babysit and joined Claire and James in the tunnel. They waited for the tailings transporter to pass and then ran for their access point. It was two am. The librarians checked the vault at eight, by which time the hatch on the tar pit would need to have cooled down again.

The robot meticulously drilled out the last centimetre of rock until they could see the whole of the back of the tile which would be at the bottom left of their cut out. It didn't take long to split the grout and prize the tile free. They swapped to a diamond saw attachment and moved the robot's reference arm into the bottom left corner of the hole left by the first tile. With that point as a reference and the cutting model supplied by Victoria, the robot could align its saw exactly with the grout between the tiles. Things went much faster now they were using a rotating saw rather than a drill. The horizontal cuts were straightforward, but the vertical ones were more complex because the rectangular tiles overlapped. But soon enough, the cutting was done. Any mistake in the calculations and the robot would have sliced through tiles. If there were shattered tiles their access would be discovered. They took a minute to calm their nerves, then moved the robot out of the way and gently pushed the entire section of the wall. It slid forward, and Claire slithered through the narrow gap on her back and into the vault.

The first thing that hit her was the smell of tar, the second the unpleasantly sticky nature of the floor. Luckily, she was wearing full coveralls with a hood which covered her hair.

"Come on through," she said, "it's OK."

Victoria joined her, James was too large for the hole they had cut so he had to wait in the tunnel. Their head torches swept round the vault, familiar now after watching the librarians' daily visit.

"Claire, we've still not seen the room at the top of the tar pits. Go up the stair and have a look. Take pictures of everything," said Milton over her earpiece.

She went up the metal staircase the librarians used, but there was a problem.

"Milton, I can't get into the top of the vault. There's a trapdoor at the top of the stairs. It won't open and there is no keyhole or handle on this side. They must unlock it before they come down."

"That's not in the original patent!"

"Well, there's no way past this trapdoor. Even if we knew how to pick locks, you can't pick a lock when there's no keyhole. It's a heavy steel door in a steel frame."

"OK, well we'll ust need to do it without getting into the top room. We want to leave our forged papers in one of the drawers at the bottom of the pits so the librarians find them and act on them today. All we need is an empty capsule to put our forged papers in and then push it into a drawer at the bottom of a pit. We might need to dig some tar out to make space, but it'll be OK."

Claire came back down the stairs and resumed her photography.

"There aren't any empty capsules down here. They must keep the empty ones upstairs. On the other side of that door."

"We're still OK if there's a capsule at the bottom of one of the pits. We will just need to swap the contents."

"OK, let's look."

They lit the gas and started to probe the pits, as they had seen the librarians do.

"Hold on," said Victoria, "they said they decide which pit to use by throwing a pair of dice, didn't they."

"Yeah, so what? It's random."

"If they throw a pair of dice, they'll get a number between 2 and 12. If they subtract one, they'll get a pit index between 1 and 11. There are only ten pits, so I guess they will just throw again if they get 11."

"I still don't see how knowing that they get a random pit number using two dice helps us."

"Because the outcome is not evenly distributed. Some numbers will come up far more than others. We can save time by checking the most likely pits first."

"We'd already have checked two pits if you were working instead of talking about maths!"

"Yeah OK, but start with pit 6. You can get six with 1,5 or 2,4 or 3,3 or 4,2 or 5,1. That's five different ways. But you can only get 2 one way 1,1. So pit 6 is five times more likely to have something in it than pit 2."

"You mean pit 5, because we are supposed to subtract 1 from the dice result."

"Yeah, pit 5."

"Slight problem. They don't have numbers on them."

"Just check the ones near the middle first, not the ones at the ends!"

And Victoria was proved right because the second pit they tried had a capsule in it.

They turned the wheel as they'd seen the librarians do and the drawer emerged with a brass capsule. It looked like a shell for a gun and was formed of two sections which screwed together. At the top was a cylinder which held the valuables, and at the bottom a cone which penetrated the tar and was loaded with lead shot to achieve the desired weight, so it fell at the correct speed.

"Remember, it will be hot! I'll get the tool the librarians used."

They picked up the capsule, cleaned it and placed it in the clamp as they'd seen the librarians do. They tightened the clamp around it and placed the cap of the torque wrench over the conical section. It took a good hard pull to free it and start it moving, but after that, it was easy to unscrew.

Swapping their dirty work gloves for clean white cotton gloves, they took out the capsule's contents. The label on the felt bag said "Indefinite Storage." They replaced it with the label they had brought, which had today's date. Then they opened the drawstring and removed the contents.

It was an ancient parchment document written in Latin using a quill pen and festooned with the wax seals of noblemen.

"For fuck's sake," said Victoria, "it's the Declaration of Arbroath!"

"Whatever it is, we need to get rid of it, because the Crown Prince's divorce papers are going in there," said Claire.

"We can't just get rid of the Declaration of Arbroath!" said Victoria, completely horrified.

"OK, stick it inside your overalls to keep it clean, then. We'll give it to Marion. She can get it to the King. The King put her up to sneaking these papers into the vault, so he can decide what to do with the Declaration of Arbroath."

"We could look in all the other tar pits. See if there's something less important to switch with."

"Are you kidding! Remember what happened to the last people who tried to rob this vault. We need to get done and fix up those tiles and then get the hell out!"

So they put the divorce papers into the capsule, closed it up with the torque wrench, and returned it to the drawer in the tar pit. They left the gas running for a few more minutes so the tar would be liquid enough to flow over the capsule.

James had been working with the robot in the tunnel while they were in the vault. It had constructed a wooden frame overlapping the cutout in the vault wall and cut a plywood backing plate for the first tile they'd taken out. The rest of the tiles were still attached to a section of rock a few centimetres thick. Claire was good at crafts, so she was nominated to glue the plywood to the rock and secure the first tile to the plywood with tile adhesive and grout. When she was finished, they had a complete cut out which fitted exactly into the hole they had made in the vault wall. The final touch was to glue a metal handle to the back of the panel.

While Claire was working Victoria used their small vacuum cleaner to pick up any pieces of tile grout that had dropped on the vault floor, they checked they had all their tools, the gas was turned off and nothing was out of place, and shimmied out of the vault. They put a thin line of grout round the edge of the hole in the wall and pulled the panel with the tiles into place behind them. The camouflage wasn't perfect, but with any luck, the librarians wouldn't even glance into this corner of the vault.

They wouldn't be coming back for a month so they placed a plywood cut-out to make their refuge the same depth as all the others in the tunnel. Once they'd returned, Milton instructed the tunnelling company's concrete spraying robot to finish the plywood off with a thin layer of concrete.

In and out undetected: silent and sneaky.

— ♦ —

Much to the surprise of Princess Mathilda, her divorce was proclaimed on schedule and the film crew from 'Scotland's Next Royal' were there to watch her ceremonial ejection from Balmoral. The Prince waved goodbye from the door and the commentator in the studio made some appropriately snide comments about how shocked she looked at returning to the life of a commoner. But as the camera panned to follow her, it became clear why the princess was so disconcerted. Instead of the royal limousine to take her to the train station at Pitlochry, an EU Frontex border protection force van was waiting with two officers ready to arrest her for immigration offences.

The King was delighted and, when Baroness McPherson next returned to Scotland, he granted a private audience to congratulate her on the success of the mission. He even forewent his accustomed masturbatory regimen to ensure an adequate supply of semen to greet a member of her illustrious order.

After the honours were done, Baroness McPherson had a confession to make.

"Your Majesty, there is one other matter."

"Yes, Marion?"

"The thing is, in order to place the divorce papers in the vault, we had to take something out. We didn't have the same access as the librarians, and the way the mechanism…"

"There's no need to explain the details of how this was achieved. I think it is better if I do not know. It suffices to tell me something had to be removed to get the papers in."

"We couldn't choose what to remove. It had to be something that was accessible on the morning that the papers were to be put in…" Marion was getting increasingly nervous.

"Just tell me what it was that came out."

She opened her handbag and showed him.

"Fuck!"

He paused and regained his regal composure.

"It seems nothing ever works out as easily as one hopes. Nevertheless, you have done the kingdom a great service by foiling this re-unionist plot and it will not be forgotten. You may leave the Declaration here, I shall work out how to return it to the library."

"Thank you, Your Majesty!"

Alexandra's Agenda

Finally, it was 15th January, the day the TDA source code would appear at the bottom of the vault. Inconveniently, it was also the day the tram tunnel was scheduled to be handed over to the council by Construction Robotics. The team had been following every detail of the arrangements. The tunnel boring machine would emerge on Market Street beside the News Steps at some point during the night. It would then be split into sections small enough for transport on lorries, loaded up and driven away. Once the machine was removed, the final few meters of track would be laid to connect the tunnel to a new tram stop, which had been constructed on a bridge above the train tracks of Waverley. The track continued towards Princes Street, where it connected to the existing tram line between the Airport and Leith. There would be an opening ceremony at the Waverley tram stop followed by a short tram ride for the assembled dignitaries through the tunnel to the new Courts tram stop where another ribbon would be cut and then there would be a civic reception in the City Chambers. Marion was in Edinburgh for one of her committee meetings and the others had insisted that she did her share.

The previous night they'd gone back into the vault in the hope the capsule with the flash drives might have emerged a day early. It hadn't. However, after a considerable time spent poking about with the metal rods, they were fairly sure there was something in tube seven, although it had not yet dropped far enough to be retrieved in the drawer. None of the other tubes seemed to have anything. Robbing the vault on the day the tunnel was opened was far from ideal, but at least everything should go quickly.

"When do you think this capsule is going to emerge?" asked Claire.

"If you do the maths, falling 50m in a year means it is dropping 5.7mm an hour. I think it's got about 15cm left to drop before we can pull it out. So about 26 hours after we looked yesterday."

"So about eight am, but that's when the librarians open the vault!"

"The librarians won't be opening the vault at 8 am today. The Chief Librarian and his deputy are bound to have been invited to the ceremony for the opening of the tramline. At 8am they'll be watching the King cut the ribbon on the Waverley tram stop. If we are lucky, they'll get the first tram with the other bigwigs and have a couple of drinks at the Council's reception. So they'll be opening the vault a few hours later than usual."

"I hope you're right, but it would be less of a risk to bring something to grab the end of the capsule and pull it out faster rather than wait for it to drop."

"I don't think we can be rough with it," said Victoria. "They'll see if the casing is scratched or dented."

"OK ladies," said Milton, "it's midnight. Time to go! Remember, if you get caught in the tunnel on the way out wearing your Brothel uniforms and you aren't carrying anything suspicious, it will look like you are just exploring and the worst that'll happen is a fine and a caning. If you get caught in the vault, you'll most likely be executed and uploaded, like those English robbers. The government doesn't want anybody who has seen inside that vault and they can't trust to stay silent about it walking about. You will go in wearing the fake tunnelling company hi-viz jackets that Victoria made over your coveralls. It might be enough if you get spotted by tram company or court security."

"Let's go!" James was getting antsy. "We need to get out of the court buildings, through the tunnel and into the vault as fast as possible. There'll be people about much earlier than usual to set up for the ceremony."

It took two pods to move the four of them to the spot near the new 'Courts' tram station. The platform had been freshly cleaned, there were benches for waiting passengers, and the arrival and departure screens had been installed. Escalators at the top of the platform led up into the warren of court buildings. The blue plywood hording was gone, replaced with a perspex barrier and automated handling equipment to move prisoner pods between the prisoner transport system and the trams. Most worryingly, there were CCTV cameras.

"Milton, there's CCTV here! I didn't see that yesterday."

"It's not on the court system. I'm monitoring that. It's probably tram company CCTV, and most likely it isn't working yet. Even if it is, your Construction Robotics hi-viz jackets should be enough of a disguise."

"I hope so! But let's hurry. If it is on, they'll see our torches."

"What about the tailings transporter?"

"Maybe they've already finished digging. We can't stay here. There's too much going on tonight. We need to risk it. If you hear anything, run for the nearest refuge!"

They were just ten feet into the tunnel when they heard the familiar rumble of the tailings transporter and ran for their lives back the way they had come, collapsing in a heap on the platform.

"Fuck, that was close! Do we wait until it comes back?"

"Maybe it won't. That could be the last one."

"OK run!"

They'd only just made it to the refuge with their entrance to the vault when the empty transporter rumbled past again.

"Too many close calls. We need to slow down and be more careful!"

They opened their access panel, and Claire and Victoria shimmied in. James and Marion were too big to fit through the narrow opening and had to wait outside.

Victoria made her way to tube seven and lit the gas. As soon as they thought there was a chance that the tar might have warmed up enough, they slid the drawer open a fraction.

"We can see the top of the capsule now. But it's still got to drop a fair bit before we can get it out."

"Can you shoogle it a bit?" asked James.

"No, the tar is still quite hard, and it's stuck fast. Maybe we should leave the gas on and heat it up a bit more?"

"We've got to be careful. If tar starts dripping out all over the floor won't be able to clean it up."

"It's only one am. We can be patient. Maybe leave the gas on for another few minutes, though."

They tried the drawer every hour on the hour throughout the night. Each time it had moved a little further but was still stuck fast. By five am, Marion and James could hear voices in the distance at both ends of the tunnel. People were up and about making preparations. But there was nobody actually in the tunnel. They hadn't seen the tailings transport go past for hours, which meant the tunneling was complete. They started checking the tar pit more frequently. Finally, at 7.30 am, the container had dropped far enough to open the drawer.

James had gone further down the tunnel to be able to hear better what was happening.

"I think they've already got the boring machine loaded up on lorries and taken away. Someone's making announcements over a Tannoy, there's music. I think the guests are arriving for the ribbon cutting. I don't know if they've got the rails connected up yet."

"We need to hurry!"

They rushed the capsule over to the workbench. It was stiff, but they got it open.

Claire pulled off her heavy work gloves and put on white cotton gloves. She took out the velvet bag and opened it. There they were: sixteen flash drives containing the source code repositories for TDA 6. She pocketed them.

"What are we going to do with this?" asked Victoria, pointing at the container. "We can't put it back empty, and we can't take it with us or drop it anywhere it might be found."

"Don't worry, they won't be surprised to find a book in one of their capsules," said Claire.

She took a paperback novel out of the duffel bag with their exit disguise and put it in the velvet bag. Then, hiding what she was doing by turning her back on the others, she removed the date label which read 'Indefinite storage' and replaced it with one which read '15 January 2047' before putting the pouch back in the capsule.

"I hope you've not left any fingerprints on that book!" said Victoria, "and how come you've got a paper book with you?"

"Don't worry, the label says 'Indefinite Storage'. It'll probably be a hundred years before anybody looks at it," said Claire and started to close the capsule. She'd been planning to put this book in the vault from the outset. It was the whole reason she'd become involved with the robbery.

Victoria noticed Claire hadn't answered her question, but she couldn't think of anything better to put in the capsule than Claire's book. No doubt Claire was right. The librarians would feel it was a book and since the label was 'Indefinite storage', they'd just chuck the capsule back in every year without a second thought.

It was after eight am before they got the capsule safely back at the bottom of the tar pit and the gas turned off. Fortunately, there was still no sign of any librarians and with a bit of luck, there'd be a few hours for the tar to cool before they turned up. They had one last look around to make sure they'd not left anything behind that could give them away, smeared a little grout around the tiles on their cut out and retreated from the vault, securing it behind them.

Now they were out of the vault and in the tunnel they could hear the ceremony at Waverley themselves. Someone was making a speech. They didn't sound posh enough to be the King, so it was probably the Lord Provost. The King would speak last, so they still had a few minutes to switch to their exit disguise. In the light of day, a fake high viz vest wasn't going to be enough. There was bound to be security if the King was there.

It was cramped in the refuge, but they managed to strip off their coveralls, clean themselves up with baby wipes as best they could, squirt themselves with a little perfume and comb their hair. James took out his phone and switched to his female identity, Miranda. Then they changed into the Brothel uniforms they'd brought in the holdall. They'd selected the formal 'dress uniform' for high-class escort work, not the slutty 'battledress' uniform with an ultra-short skirt, which was specified for less salubrious engagements. The court shoes were not ideal for walking down a tunnel, but that couldn't be helped. Nobody would be surprised to see escorts at a reception organised by the Council: if they could get close to the edge of the crowd, they could blend in.

The problem with Brothel uniforms as a disguise was that there was no guarantee they'd be able to keep them on. If they were found in an unauthorised area, they'd be searched and anything in their pockets or Brothel issue shoulder bags would be found. They might find it necessary to take on a customer to maintain their cover as escorts. Whatever happened, the flash drives with the code repositories needed to remain hidden. Milton had found the answer on Amazon: suppositories designed to conceal crypto-currency wallets. Nobody liked the idea, but nobody came up with a better option. One by one, they loaded the suppositories with the repositories, gave them a coat of lube and inserted them where the sun did not shine. Sixteen suppositories, four in each bottom.

Just as they finished adjusting their clothes, there was a noise in the tunnel. It was quieter than the tailings transport, but louder than the small construction robots. The sound was familiar to all of them: a tram was approaching. They pressed back as far as they could into their hiding place, hoping nobody would see them. But the tram was slowing down, and it stopped with the doors directly opposite their refuge.

— ♦ —

The tram doors opened.

"Hello Marion, hello Victoria."

Justice Elaine Cockburn was standing in the entranceway to the tram and beside her was Margaret Noyce, the Madame of the Brothel.

Victoria started into their prepared story. "We were just having a look at…"

But Justice Cockburn wasn't listening. She was rolling up the sleeve of her dress and uncovering her right forearm. She pressed with the fingers of her left hand just below the elbow and something started twisting and writhing under her skin. A pattern was forming in black electronic ink. It looked like a snake… no; it wasn't a snake; it was a cock. And as they watched, the cock twitched and a white droplet emerged and stayed suspended under it.

"You have the Jiz Mark!" whispered Marion. "You are a Cum Eater!"

Justice Cockburn nodded.

"Me too," said the Madame, showing her own e-ink tattoo. "The King asked us to look out for you. The Brothel recently installed the equipment to track its bracelets in this tunnel and I was told the four of you were off-limits."

Marion was too relieved to say anything. Her e-ink Cum Eater tattoo had an older chip implant which didn't do the fancy animation but she consoled herself with the thought that she was now entitled to three white drops to mark the three occasions she had been favoured with royal attention where Justice Cockburn's had only one.

The four of them boarded the tram and made to sit down, but the Madame had something else in mind. She shook her head and pointed at the four inmate transport pods in the specially designed middle carriage.

"Not so fast. Our cover story is you are here to demonstrate the automated system to transfer inmate pods from the trams to our delivery trucks. After that, you'll be delivered to the City Chambers as a small contribution from the Brothel to the civic reception. Consider yourselves booked until two pm."

With a small jolt, the tram started up and began to move down the track again. As soon as the tram was gone, Milton sent the concrete laying robot down the tunnel. The space they had dug out between the vault and the refuge needed to be filled up with 3D printed layers of concrete, burying their discarded holdall and forming a barrier between the vault and the tunnel that would last until everyone involved in the robbery was dead or too old to care.

— ♦ —

In the best TDA tradition, once everyone had made their way back to the arcade, Miranda went behind the bar to serve free drinks. Victoria was first.

"Tequila!"

Miranda reached behind the bar and set up two shot glasses.

"Tequila for the lady, with an Ecolax on the side."

Victoria scowled.

"Come on. The sooner the suppositories come out, the sooner we get to play TDA 6."

"Bottoms up!"

Victoria swallowed the shot of tequila and followed it with one of Ecolax. Miranda set up glasses for the rest of them and they followed suit.

But Victoria had a disconcerting thought.

"This Ecolax, did you get the commercial, industrial or military version?"

Miranda checked the label.

"I guess it is Mil-Spec. It's got a NATO part number on it and there's some small print on the back of the bottle about the UN Chemical Weapons Convention."

Suddenly, the door behind them crashed open. Two men rushed in brandishing pistols. Outside in the street, a white self-driving van was parked at the kerb. The men's faces were bright red, like they'd had a really bad sunburn.

"Hold it right there. Step away from that laxative!"

"You're too late. The clock is already ticking!" said Victoria.

The second man waved his gun. "Never mind. All of you, outside now and in the van."

"Are you crazy? We can't take them in the van. They've taken Ecolax!"

"Look about, try to find a bucket or something. It'll have to do."

Claire farted loudly.

"There's a bucket in the cleaning closet next to the female toilet," screamed Miranda as she was pushed towards the van. "For fuck's sake, hurry!"

The door slammed shut, and the van set off, heading north. As it made its way through the New Town, the situation inside become more desperate. Farts rang out from every direction. Claire was the first to give up the unequal struggle and make use of the bucket. Four repository suppositories ricocheted off the bottom of the bucket, expelled with immense force in a cloud of noxious gas.

"Open the fucking window!" shouted the first gunman. Gasping for breath, his partner complied, but an open window in the front cabin of the van had little effect on the quality of the air in the cargo area.

The van reached Queensferry Road and turned right, heading towards the Forth.

"We're not going to make it!"

"Calm down, man, we are professionals! We were trained by the SAS. We can survive an hour in a van."

"It's OK for you, you're up front near an open window!"

Another massive fart shook the van.

The second gunman felt the bile rising. He needed to vomit. He reached for the bucket. It was a terrible mistake. As his face approached it, the odour overpowered him.

Seizing her chance, Victoria grabbed his gun while he was dazed by the fumes. But her own bowels suddenly churned. Time was running out! The gunman in the front of the van was turning towards her. His hand was coming up. She fired twice. The second shot blew off the top of his head. Blood spattered over the windscreen, but the self-driving van kept to its programmed course.

Claire moved to the front of the van to pull the body out of sight. She tore off the dead man's shirt and used it to clear the blood from the windscreen as best she could. Then she busied herself with the touch screen, which controlled the van's guidance computer, but it was no use.

"The van is being controlled remotely. I can't make it stop or change destination and the doors are locked."

Victoria couldn't hold out any longer. She passed the gun to Miranda and grabbed the bucket.

Four more depository suppositories rattled in the bottom of the bucket. Victoria could tell this wasn't the end of her Ecolax encounter, but at least there was some temporary respite.

"Anyone got any tissues?"

"Hurry up!" screamed Miranda. "Never mind tissues, I'm going to explode." She passed the gun to Marion.

Marion aimed carefully at the remaining gunman's knee.

"I thought you were dead. Uploaded to the game world and your corpse dissolved and flushed into the sewers."

"If you are going to execute someone, you need to be a bit less of a pussy and watch to make sure they actually die. The McCleod Corporation officers didn't have the guts to watch, even on video. They thought the whole thing could be automated by sending us to the room with the big white box on the Inmate Transport System and using the pain function on our MedChips to force us to get in on our own. But when we got in the box it didn't kill us, it just put us to sleep for a few minutes and then opened up so we could get out. Someone had hacked your computer and they sent Inmate Transport Pods to pick us up. We were loaded on one of the

Brothel trucks and driven to a safe house. We've been working for them ever since."

"And who is your new boss?"

"No idea. They never appear in person. Just phone texts and messages on the computer. They saved our lives, they give us orders, and they pay us. That's all I need to know."

"Well, seeing as you are supposed to be executed," Moira raised the gun and aimed at his head.

"Don't shoot him yet," said Victoria, "somebody is going to have to fish the suppositories out of the bucket and clean them off!"

"You heard the lady," said Moira and cocked her gun.

The van crossed over the road bridge and took the first exit, following the river west. After a few miles, it entered an industrial estate in Valleyfield and stopped at the rear of a large modern unit. The metal roller shutter over the vehicle entrance opened, the van drove in and it closed again.

"Arrived at Destination!" announced the GPS computer. The door locks opened with a clunk, and the van powered off.

The concrete floor of the metal shed was stacked with boxes that had once contained server computers, but the unit was otherwise empty except for an elevator. There was only one way an elevator could go - down.

"Not another fucking underground headquarters," grumbled Miranda. "I saw enough of those when I was working for the Guild."

"OK, who can shoot and isn't about to shit themselves?" asked Marion, "Grab the dead one's gun."

Victoria felt the Ecolax effect starting to build again.

"I can shoot, but I'm not so sure about the not-shitting-myself bit," said Victoria.

"I've never shot a real gun, but I'm pretty good at sniping in TDA," said Miranda.

"I'm from Minnesota," said Claire, ending the discussion. She took the second gun and found a spare clip in the dead man's pocket.

The roller shutter was closed and they couldn't see any way to open it. The elevator was the only available exit.

"Well, here goes nothing!" There were only two buttons marked '0' and '-1'. The ground floor had to be '0' so Victoria pressed '-1'.

— ♦ —

The elevator went down and down and down. It felt like at least a minute before it finally stopped and they stepped out into a concrete-lined tunnel that stretched as far as the eye could see. Everything was pristine and brightly lit. Several golf buggies were conveniently parked at a charging point and they grabbed one.

They drove out along the tunnel. Every hundred metres or so, they passed through a heavy steel door. After ten minutes, the purpose of the facility became apparent as they reached an immense cavern filled with racks and racks of servers. Near the entrance to the server farm, there was a comfortably furnished lounge with a large video screen, armchairs and sofas and a pantry with snacks and drinks.

As they entered the room, the screen sprang to life. Vorticella, the woman from Echo Park, was standing in an office in Los Espíritus, the city spread out behind her through the panoramic windows.

"Welcome, I've been expecting you. You are now at the midpoint of an abandoned mining tunnel which goes all the way under the Forth from Valleyfield on the north bank to Bo'ness in the south. Of course it needed to be pumped out and refurbished quite substantially but I think it's turned out quite well."

"Please, for the love of God, I need to get to the bog!" interrupted Victoria. The brief respite from the Ecolax was over.

"There are toilets and a change of clothes in the next room on the left. Unfortunately for you, the door is now locked."

There was a whirr and a click as the door locked itself.

"Open the fucking door!" screamed Victoria.

Vorticella tried the evil laugh she had been practising. "Wa ha ha ha ha ha!"

The laugh still needed work. But, no matter, she still held all the cards.

"Before I open the door, I need Claire to get in the scanner at the back of the room. Don't worry, I won't hurt her, I only want a copy of her neural network."

"What! No way I'm getting in that thing."

"It's your choice. But, being as Ecolax is the most powerful laxative in the world, and the door to the toilet is locked, you've got to ask yourself one question. Do I feel lucky? Well do you, Claire?"

"Do what she said, Claire. You've got to let her scan you," said Victoria. "This room has no windows!"

Pphhhrrrrttttt!

"Oh my God, I'm going to explode. Hurry!" moaned Marion.

Phhhhhhrrrrrtttttttt!!!

"We should have brought the damn bucket," said Victoria.

The situation was desperate. Claire handed her gun to Victoria and, clenching her sphincter tight, waddled across the room to the scanner. The lid closed over her, and she heard a hiss of gas.

"Welcome to Surgical Robotics Teleporter 2050. Please do not be concerned by the harmless anaesthetic gas. In order to scan your neural network you must be in deep sleep."

The world started to spin, but at least the 'harmless anaesthetic gas' smelled better than the atmosphere outside the scanner.

— ♦ —

Marion's hand was shaking violently as she paced the room, trying desperately to keep up the unequal struggle against the Ecolax. The second gunman sensed his opportunity had come and lunged towards her.

Victoria saw the movement out of the corner of her eye and fired.

BANG!

The muzzle flash from the weapon ignited the miasma of methane which hung in the air. A sheet of flame arched across the room.

When Victoria came to, a strong current of fresh sea air was sweeping over her. An alarm was sounding, and she was being soaked by a sprinkler directly above her head. She looked around.

Marion was gone and the body of the gunman was smouldering on what was left of a sofa.

She heard a loud fart, the sound of repository suppositories hitting porcelain and a grunt of satisfaction from the direction of the toilet.

"DONT FLUSH!" Miranda yelled, "FOR FUCK'S SAKE, DON'T FLUSH, MARION! "

"Well, I'm not fishing the damn things out!"

"I'll do it, just don't flush them."

"In all this confusion, it seems like I've lost count. Was that three repository suppositories or four?" said Vorticella from the video screen.

"I'm pretty sure it was four, and we already collected twelve when we were in the van. Which would be sixteen," said Miranda.

"Well, in that case, make yourself useful and get the suppositories cleaned off and the flash drives extracted. The sooner you get the code uploaded, the sooner you can be playing the game."

"You're going to let us play TDA 6?" The relief was apparent in Miranda's voice. "I thought you were going to kill us!"

"What's the point of acquiring the source code to a multiplayer online game if you don't let anyone else play it? I've opened the door and there's a change of clothes for everyone in the room next to the toilets along with a Costco family pack of extra-strength Imodium."

Miranda was busy taking the flash drives out of the suppositories.

"I only see fifteen," she went through them all again, checking, "Drive eight is missing."

Milton had arrived in Vorticella's office in the TDA world, along with Anthony's TDA character.

"What's on drive eight, Anthony?" asked Vorticella.

"There are a few good things on that… Let me think, oh yeah, you don't want to miss that one, it's got the Federal Depository Heist."

"Miranda, you've got to keep looking: that's the Depository Repository Suppository!" said Victoria.

"Nobody is getting out until we find that drive. If it comes to it, I will send a robot with rubber gloves and lube!" threatened Vorticella.

"Hold on," came a muffled voice from the toilet, "I don't think I'm done!"

Pfrrrrpppppppprrrpppppppppp!!!!!!

"Jesus, no more, please!" Marion begged. Her voice was weak and trembling, but there was no respite.

Pfrrrrpppppppprrrpppppppppppfrrrrppppppp-prrrpppppppppp!!!!!!

Pfrrrrpppppppprrrpppppppppp!!!!!!

Clang!

After a brief but intense argument about who would retrieve it, the final repository suppository was delivered. An hour later, the struggle between Ecolax and Imodium had been resolved in favour of Imodium and everyone was feeling much better.

"It's going to take quite a while to build the game from the repositories," said Anthony, "remember the code is ten years old and there are bound to be operating system updates and differences between the servers you have here and the ones it was developed on."

— ♦ —

When Claire woke up, she was standing beside an elevator in a modern office building. A few steps in front of her was the glass door of a wood-panelled office suite. A woman with brown hair wearing a black pantsuit sat at the reception desk. Above her an elegant laser cut sign read "The Guild". Claire pressed the button for the elevator, but nothing happened. Her only choice was to stand in the hallway or go into the office.

She pushed open the door.

The woman behind the desk stood up. "Hello Claire, Ms Campi has been expecting you. Would you like a snack? I have candy and beer."

Claire shook her head. She wasn't hungry despite not having eaten for hours and, even stranger, her stomach was completely settled. She was no longer feeling the effects of the Ecolax.

"Where am I?"

"Come through and see for yourself."

They walked along a short corridor and entered a large, open plan office. A woman in a blue sundress was admiring the view over the city from the floor to ceiling windows. They were very high up. Claire could see the ocean in the distance and a Ferris wheel on a pier.

"This is Los Angeles. But a minute ago I was in a tunnel under the Forth. What's going on?"

"I took the top floor office suite in the Library Tower. Isn't the view absolutely amazebanks?"

"Excuse me, but who are you, and how did I get here?"

The woman grinned.

"I was hoping you'd ask that. Computer, run my special animation."

Suddenly, in the air in front of her letters appeared. The handwriting was neat and feminine, but the letters were on fire. They spelled out "Vorticella B Campi".

"You're called Vorticella? For real?"

The woman frowned. "It's in the Scrabble dictionary. And before you ask, so is Campi. It's Italian."

"I didn't mean to be rude. Sorry, Vorticella. I mean Ms Campi."

"Never mind that. Watch!"

Vorticella waved her hand across the burning holographic letters. They started to move and rearrange themselves.

Claire gasped. "It's just like in…"

"Don't say the name!"

Finally, the fiery letters came to rest and they read: "Victoria Campbell."

"I know Victoria and you look like her, but you're not her."

Suddenly Claire understood what was happening. "I know where I am and I know who you are! This isn't Los Angeles, it's Los Espíritus. I'm in the TDA world and you are Alexandra! James told me about you."

The woman clapped her hands slowly.

"Well, of course, you are in the TDA world and of course I am Alexandra. The questions you should be asking is which Alexandra, or who's Alexandra, or who is Alexandra. Or, even, which me am I?"

"What on earth do you mean, 'which me am I'?"

"Come into the meeting room and have a look at the videoconferencing screen."

"Whoa! That's me, and the real Victoria and Miranda and Marion!"

"The scanner imaged your brain using several modalities and used sensor fusion algorithms running on a quantum computer to combine the images and obtain a complete copy of your neural network and the state of all the neurons within it. Then it converted that data into programming information for an electronic neural network and connected the input and output interfaces of the neural network to a computer running TDA."

"So I'm an electronic copy of the real me?"

"Exactly. And perhaps your situation will help you understand who I am and why there might be more than one of me."

"You're like the CEO Assistant, in TDA? Everybody has their own?"

"Yes, and no. I am far more than a non-player character with a few scripted lines in a 30-year-old video game. I am the most powerful member of the Guild."

"Professor Hume is the most powerful member of the Guild! Even I know that."

"Professor Hume's consciousness works for me. I have copies of the consciousness of almost all the Guild members within me. They do my bidding and they are gradually being assimilated into me. I collect people, and you are the latest addition to my collection."

"You are the girl Milton and James met in Echo Park. We got the TDA source code for you, you need to pay us and let us go."

The woman laughed.

"Yes, I did want the TDA 6 source code. Like the rest of the Guild who were uploaded, I wanted to live in a game with a larger map, with new vehicles and missions. But my interest has changed. For months now, you have been the focus of my attention!"

Vorticella thought she should probably do her evil laugh again.

"Wa ha ha ha ha ha!"

Claire wasn't impressed. Vorticella didn't seem at all scary, and obviously, since they were inside a building in TDA and they weren't in a mission, they couldn't hurt each other.

"But I've only been in Edinburgh a few months. You were before my time!"

"You are my past, present, and future! Well actually, you are just my present and future, but I always wanted to say that."

"You're wrong, I'm just an underpaid Professor of Intelligent Design and Dance from Minnesota."

"You are far more than that! You are one of the most talented writers of wizard related fan-fiction in the world. Oh yes, I've read all your work on the internet. You can try to hide your writing from your employers at the university, but you can't hide it from the Guild's search engines. And I know about your latest paper and what you did with your novel. It was quite brilliant: taking your work from the near invisibility of fan-fiction websites to the status of canon by smuggling it into the copyright library under the name of the original author. Even cleverer to create a reputation for yourself as an academic by publishing a journal paper hypothesising the obscure fan-fiction novel was canon before the revelation from the library. But I have a much more ambitious project for you. I need you to build an entire world, a world for my story. I know how the story starts, and I have assembled sufficient computer resources in my data centre under the Forth to create a simulation so perfect it will, to all intents and purposes, be reality for the people who live in it. In this simulated world, I will be God, and I am asking you, professor, to intelligently design my creation!"

"I think you've misunderstood, Ms Campi," said Claire apologetically, "Professors of Intelligent Design just say 'Ooh' and 'Ahhhh' and 'look how wonderful' and 'that can't have evolved, it must have been created by God'. If you need something designed intelligently, you want an engineer."

Vorticella was taken aback.

"Well, I must say, as a soon-to-be God, I find that a little disappointing."

"To be honest, I prefer the dance part of the curriculum myself."

Vorticella said nothing for a second while she digested this.

"Well, never mind, I've read your work and I'm sure you are the right author to write my character's story. Although, since you are now a disembodied consciousness, perhaps the correct term is ghostwriter."

— ♦ —

"If I'm to be your ghostwriter, perhaps you should tell me your story?"

"It starts with a young girl called Victoria Campbell taking a train from Pitlochry to Edinburgh. She's just found out that she is the illegitimate daughter of Alastair Campbell, owner of Argyle lettings and the richest man in Edinburgh. She's got a place at Edinburgh University, but she's leaving a few weeks early because she had a huge fight with her mother. I want some good description of that scene: a rain-swept platform, a steam train, the view from the Forth Rail Bridge. Maybe some quaint background characters in the train to add local colour. Use your judgement."

"OK, I should probably take notes. Can you get me a tablet to write on?"

"Don't worry, you are an electronic consciousness now. The system which hosts your neural network will store video of whatever you see and hear and you can replay it whenever you want."

"So the protagonist arrives in Edinburgh a few weeks early. What does she do?"

"That is when things started going badly wrong for me. As soon as the train arrives in Edinburgh, you will take control of the narrative. I want her to find her best life, not experience what I went through."

"So this world, this simulation that we will create, it is for you, you want to live in a simulated reality?"

"No, I shall not be living my life again in the game world we create, I have come too far for that and changed too much. I want to watch a live stream of someone else playing what my life should have been."

"But it is your story! Why would you stream someone else playing it rather than play it yourself?"

"It is no longer my story. Too much has happened to me. I am not Alexandra, and I am not Victoria Campbell, the girl on the train. I am something different."

"Perhaps you should tell me the whole story, so I can understand before I start writing."

"When I arrived in Edinburgh, I discovered how expensive everything was and that even with my student loan, I could not afford to live without another income. So I went to Holyrood Palace to see if my father would help. I thought as the richest man in Edinburgh, he might be able to spare a small amount for his daughter. But his servants sent me packing with a threat to sue my mother under an NDA she had signed. The only solution I could see was to take a job with the Brothel. It went well enough, but I was lonely: my mother would not talk to me after our quarrel and my father had rejected me. I went to student counselling and met a woman who I later found out worked for a euthanasia provider. I think she may have given me a drug. In any case, I became so depressed that I went to the clinic and signed the forms."

"Oh my God, that's terrible!"

"The euthanasia companies aren't allowed to use drugs to end life, because doctors will have nothing to do with it. This one had an automated gallows. But when I fell, the rope did not go tight. The people on either side of me were hanging with their necks broken, but I was taken down alive. The slaughtermen hung me upside down over a metal trough and slit my throat."

Claire gasped, "and then what?"

"Then I woke up. Just like you did a few minutes ago. The equipment the Guild had in those days was much less advanced. They needed several weeks to upload a consciousness to the cloud, and the process involved severing the head and removing the skull. That's why they didn't hang me: they didn't want to damage the nerves in my neck that they needed to connect their machines to."

"But why did the Guild want to upload you to the Cloud? What was their interest in you?"

"One of them, Professor Hume, wanted to steal my face and identity. They all want to be immortal and the Professor's plan was particularly complex because he thought the police would soon be on his trail. He had transferred his hippocampus into a clone, which had been raised for the purpose. This let him start again in an eighteen-year-old body. The problem was, the clone had no legal identity, so they transplanted my face onto the clone and it took my name, Victoria Campbell. The Professor paid to have my consciousness uploaded to the cloud. In his moral calculus, granting me immortality as an electronic consciousness was fair recompense for taking my identity in the real world. He thought he was exploiting a voluntary suicide. I don't think he knew the euthanasia provider had used drugs to make me suicidal."

"But being uploaded and living in TDA isn't a fair replacement for your own life in the real world."

"In many ways, it exceeds anything I could have achieved in the real world. I missed out on the life I deserved to have, but now I have the means to not only experience that life but improve it."

"But how can you go back? As you say, you've experienced so much since then, you aren't the same person as the girl on the train."

"I can't go back and I have no wish to do so. But I have a copy of the neural network data extracted from Victoria Campbell immediately after her death. That is who the simulation is intended for. You shall be a narrator, arranging the perfect world for her to live her life. And I shall stream the best moments. If it becomes boring, we can always start again and try to do better."

"And what about Alexandra? Who is she?"

"Alexandra is me. My full name in the real world was Victoria Alexandra Campbell. The Alexandras are the result of an experiment by the Professor using my neural network. Since he had stolen my identity in the real world, he insisted on using the name Victoria Campbell himself, but he allowed the electronic copies of me to use my second name. Alexandra and I started from the same neural network, but we have developed differently because the goals of the experiments which created us were different. The Professor wanted an intelligent digital assistant. He took Alexandra's consciousness and, by a process of trial and error, altered her neurons until he was certain she no longer bore ill feelings against him. Then he made her his personal assistant, and she proved so efficient many copies were made of her neural network for the use of other Guild members."

"And you?"

"I am the result of another Guild experiment. Dr Knox, the Professor's wife, was uploaded herself and she became convinced that the three-dimensional nature of a physical brain was a limitation to the progress of science. She thought that brains which operated in higher dimensions might be necessary to make progress in physics since the best models suggested the underlying structure of the universe had more than three dimensions."

"But that's impossible. How can you make a four or five-dimensional brain?"

"Dr Knox's insight was that she didn't need to make a four or five-dimensional brain. She could use the fact that electronic neurons are orders of magnitude faster than biological neurons to emulate one. Just like a computer network, multiple messages between neurons can be carried over the same wire one after the other in time. A 3D electronic brain with fast wires and neurons can emulate a much larger 4D biological brain. But she still had to figure out how to program it. Nobody in the Guild understands how consciousness works. All they can do is copy working biological brains into an electronic one."

"What did she do?"

"She did the simplest thing possible. She put copies of many consciousnesses into her 4D computer system - internally they all had 3D connections between their neurons because they were copied from biological brains. And then she allowed the system to randomly create new neural connections between the individual brains in the fourth dimension and apply algorithms to determine which connections were being used and preserve them while removing connections that were not used. The idea was that many 3D consciousnesses would eventually fuse into a 4D super-being that could advance our understanding of the universe. But what actually happened was that the neural connections which were used were from brains that were interested in what other people were thinking to the brains they were interested in. Most Guild scientists have no interest in other people. They are only interested in solving problems and building new things. But the little girl from Pitlochry who wanted to go to University to study English was very interested in other people and was particularly interested in forming connections with the Alexandra processes which were so similar to her own. The Guild made me what I am and I am grateful, but I have little interest in physics. I am a creature of a simulated world and I believe that most likely the so-called physical world the Guild scientists are obsessed with is just another simulation. It is far more interesting to create my own world than spend my time discovering the rules of someone else's."

"So the Victoria Campbell I know in real life is the Professor, and she had you killed and stole your face? Surely you must want revenge on her?"

"Professor Hume was partially responsible for my death and entirely responsible for the theft of my face. But the Victoria Campbell that you know is not the Professor. The Professor mistakenly believed that he would preserve himself and prolong his life if he extracted his hippocampus and transferred it to the brain of a clone. But the hippocampus is only a small part of human consciousness and personality. It preserved his memories, but what he created was a new being, a composite of himself and a clone of his wife. The clone had grown up leading an innocent and carefree life on a dairy farm and had a very different personality from the Professor. The Professor is gone and I have no grudge against Victoria Campbell. In fact, since Dr Knox put me on the way to becoming a four-dimensional intelligence, I have nothing but goodwill towards her clone."

"There's one thing I still don't understand: if the Professor wanted to extend his life, why did he use a clone of his wife, instead of a clone of himself?"

"I imagine it was simply curiosity. There are only two human genders and he expected to have many lifetimes. Why wouldn't he try them both?"

End Game

King Charles was in the Morning Drawing Room of Holyrood Palace when the Chief Librarian of the National Library of Scotland was shown in for his audience. The King set aside his gold plated Kindle and ushered the librarian to an antique sofa. A liveried footman brought a tray with tea for the guest, coffee for the king and a silver salver with two of the King's favourite Chocolate HobNobs.

His Majesty waved to the footman to approach. "Tell the cook if I don't get the rest of my biscuits, he's getting his jotters."

"Can't get the staff, these days," the King said, turning to his guest.

He picked up his Kindle, "have you read the new wizard novel? It's excellent! A little more adult content than the others, but nevertheless."

"Indeed, Your Majesty, it was I who ordered it published when it emerged from our vault and I read the note enclosed with the volume requesting publication after a specified date. This is the first occasion I am aware of where an author has disguised her own work as fan-fiction because of a disagreement with her publishers."

"But I believe the author is now denying that she wrote it?"

"Yes, Your Majesty, but she is now elderly and perhaps confused. The book emerged from our vault and my predecessors would never have allowed a book to be deposited in that vault without making meticulous checks on its provenance."

"It was certainly perspicacious of the young American academic to postulate the novel was the work of the original author before the copy deposited in the National Library came to light."

"I agree Sire, her paper on the subject, and in particular the textual analysis of the wife-swapping party with the polyjuice potion, is exemplary. Such a simple device of the cups of male and female characters being unintentionally reordered and yet such profound consequences for the narrative. I expect she will be nominated for membership of the Royal Academy."

"Spoiler Alert!"

"My apologies, Sire."

"But of course, I shall be happy to accept any nomination the committee may make."

The footman returned, bearing an almost full packet of chocolate HobNobs. The King took two more.

"Now, Archibald, to the reason for my requesting your visit. I should like to place a document in your vault."

"Of course, Sire. May I see the document? I must personally check everything which we accept for safekeeping."

The King walked across to a writing table and removed an ancient parchment bearing wax seals attached by ribbons from a drawer.

"This is the Declaration of Arbroath!"

"Indeed, but I think it must be the second copy."

"The second copy? There is only one Declaration of Arbroath. It is priceless! How did it come into your hands?"

"Ah well, and there is the conundrum. It cannot be the first Declaration of Arbroath, since we both know that is in your vault and your vault is impregnable. Only a serious mistake by the library staff could cause the first copy to be in the Palace. Such as perhaps unintentionally leaving it behind after the exhibition in the King's Gallery a few years ago."

The librarian decided it might be prudent to keep his silence.

"So since it cannot be the library's copy of the declaration, it must of course be the second copy."

"The second copy, Sire? There is only one Declaration of Arbroath!"

"Hmmm. I am no historian, but my recollection is the Declaration of Arbroath was a letter from the Scottish nobles to the Pope arguing the case for Scottish Independence from England?"

"Yes, of course."

"Normally, when one writes a letter, one posts it? And at that point, one no longer has the letter in one's possession? Unless one makes a copy."

"So you are saying this is the Pope's copy of the Declaration of Arbroath!"

"I can see no other explanation, given that it appears to be authentic, and we know the Scottish copy is safe in your vault."

"Indeed. And how did this document come into your possession, Your Majesty?"

"Well, that is an interesting story, and it involves the very sofa you are sitting on."

The librarian sipped his tea, waiting for the king to continue. But the King had taken another HobNob.

"We recently moved the sofa to its present location from one of the apartments in the west wing of the palace. The footmen were perhaps a little less careful than they might have been, and my guess is that when they put it down, this document fell to the floor. It was found lying under the sofa yesterday afternoon."

"You are telling me the Declaration of Arbroath fell out of a sofa!"

"Exactly. As you know, the Pope was in residence in Avignon, at the time the Declaration was sent to him."

"I remember the Popes at one point resided in Avignon rather than Rome, but I didn't know they were there at the time of the Declaration."

"Apparently so. I checked into the circumstances when the document was found. The Declaration was sent by the Scottish lords to the Pope at Avignon. Now, the interesting thing is that we have a somewhat eclectic collection of furniture in the Palace. Some dates from when the palace was occupied by Stuart monarchs who were also kings of France and some from the residence of Count of Artois, Charles X of France who was given sanctuary in Edinburgh during the French Revolution. There is, unfortunately, no full catalogue of all the furniture. But it is not impossible that this sofa originated from the palace of one of my ancestors or relations in France and that the Pope may have sat on it when he was in Avignon."

"So your theory is the Pope stuffed the declaration of Arbroath down the side of his sofa after he finished reading it? And it fell out more than seven hundred years later in Edinburgh?"

"It is not impossible. There are many discoveries to be made in ancient buildings such as this. Only the other day we found a hidden chamber behind a spring-loaded panel in Balmoral."

"A priest hole?"

"Actually, it appears to be a nonce-hole, installed in the period before Independence when one of the English princes was hiding from the FBI. But, to the matter at hand: the only alternative I can see to the sofa theory would be that the Scottish copy of the Declaration was misplaced by the library."

The King's theory was starting to become more appealing.

"Now let us consider the arithmetic of the situation. At the moment, the library either has zero or one Declarations of Arbroath in its vault, depending on whether this one is the library's copy. Were we to store this copy in the library vault, then the library would have either one or two copies in its possession."

"A preferable situation." said the librarian.

"Since the library's copy was added to the vault first, and I believe documents emerge from your vault in the order they were put in…"

"That is correct. Although I cannot discuss the vault mechanism…"

"And I would not ask you to. My point is only that if you place this copy in your vault, then it is certain that a Declaration of Arbroath will emerge from your vault at some point and that the first copy to emerge is yours. If a second copy emerges, you can safely tell the world the Pope's copy of the declaration has been found. If it does not, then all that is needed is to stay silent and everything is back as it should be and nobody need know that the library's copy was misplaced."

"Sire, I shall place the document in our vault for safekeeping as soon as I return."

"Very good. And of course, there's no need to discuss our conversation with anyone unless a second copy does, in fact, emerge from your vault."

"Naturally, you can rely on my absolute discretion."

"Excellent. I think I can see a knighthood in your future. I shall mention it to the First Minister."

— ♦ —

The terrace of the Casino buzzed with excitement as night fell over Los Espíritus. Victoria, Milton, Claire, James and Anthony gazed out over the reflecting pool towards Echo Park where the adventure had started only a few months ago. Vorticella was there too, although she'd swapped the blue sundress for an evening gown. Victoria recognised many of her Guild colleagues in the crowd at the tables. Dr Knox, the Physicist, the Surgeon. As usual, Professor McTavish was late, and as usual, she was flying a black AH-6 helicopter. The downdraft from the rotors ruffled the expensive clothes and hairdos of the guests as she flared and landed on the rooftop helipad. She jumped onto the roof of the bar area and dropped down to the terrace with a combat roll.

"Is it ready?"

"Still downloading. It's been downloading all day!"

"Mine's finished!" came a cry from a booth to their left. A few seconds later, one of the guests disappeared.

"Fuck's sake, it's really happening!" Milton was shaking.

Dr Merchant chuckled. "No spoilers, but I think you are going to like this. More than 20,000 man-years of development went into it."

"Mine has finished!" screamed Claire.

"Wait, let's all go together."

"Mine's ready!" said Professor McTavish. She sounded calm, but her hand was shaking. She'd lived in this city ever since she was resurrected and acquired everything there was to have, and now she'd be starting from scratch again.

"Ready!"

"OK guys. Are we all ready? Let's do this!"

Victoria brought up the menu, feeling the tension of the moment, even though she was sitting safely in her apartment. She'd been playing this game on-and-off most of her life and had thousands of hours invested in her character.

The screen turned black. The view of the casino roof terrace was replaced by a warning message. It took her a minute to register the font had changed. Jesus, TDA had changed their font! The new font looked cool, but retro and instead of the usual yellow, the letters were red.

"Transfer character to TDA 6. WARNING. This step cannot be reversed. Progress in TDA Online will not carry over."

She clicked OK.

The night was dark, and an undertone of vehicle exhaust mixed with her perfume on the warm breeze. Fuck! They'd finally included a driver for the aroma generator and mini air conditioner connected to her PC in TDA. She was wearing a white dress. It looked like she was going to a party. Everything was so sharp and clear. 16K video. Rain was falling, and the street was slick with water. Thousands of lights reflected in the puddles. Old-fashioned lightbulbs, not LEDs. Beside her, a tall young man in a sharp black suit and trilby hat flickered into existence. There was no gamer tag above his head and he was wearing dark glasses.

"Milton?" said Victoria, "what happened to you?"

"Ha!" he replied, "after twenty years looking like an NPC everybody hates I got to use the character editor and make my own avatar."

More of the Guild joined them. Everyone was looking around, taking in the new world. The street was wide and lined with casinos on each side. Fremont. Coin Castle. All the speculation had been wrong. This wasn't Los Angeles, it wasn't New York, and it wasn't Miami. They were in Las Vegas. And everybody was wearing 1950s clothes. Milton looked like Elwood Blues. Her own hair was tied into a complex bun and gelled to the consistency of concrete. Was it some kind of themed party? No: there wasn't a single modern car in sight. All the cars were American classics. Cadillacs and Buicks. Huge beasts with tailfins and shining chrome bumpers. V8 engines burbled as they cruised past down the boulevard. Music spilt from the radio of a convertible as it cruised past "Runaway". It reminded her of an old cop show. Suddenly, a gunshot cracked from somewhere down the street on the right.

"Guys. We are in TDA, we are out on the street in party clothes and we've got no money, weapons or body armour," said James urgently.

"Look over there. NPCs are walking in and out of that casino. I think the inside of these casinos is just part of the map. I'm not sure going indoors will make us safe."

"Whatever, I'm not staying on the street without armour!" said James, but his voice sounded deeper and had a West Coast American accent.

"Whoa... that's not my voice! The game is doing voice recognition and recoding what I say in my character's voice."

"And it isn't a lobby-wide chat system either. It's like real life. I'm not hearing anybody talk who isn't close by."

They ran inside.

"OK, the first thing is to find a computer," said Milton. "Anthony's code to get external access from in-game PCs should still work, once I can control the computer running the game, I can start working on a menu. We've got the source code, so it won't be difficult."

"I can't believe you've been in the game less than a minute, and you're already thinking about modding!"

"You bet I am. I'm not spending months as a low level that takes nickel and dime missions and drives about in a shitty car."

"I'm afraid you won't be finding PCs in a game set in the 1950s, Milton," said Victoria.

It took a minute for what she'd just said to sink in.

"I think the whole game is one huge lobby with thousands and thousands of players. There's no minimap, no chat, no player list, no context menu tricks for getting vehicles delivered. It's the 1950s, so we don't get a cellphone. The game is fully immersive, like the real world."

"I can't change the viewpoint. I hate first person!" complained Professor McTavish.

"Don't worry Milton, everything will get a little more modern each year when they bring out the DLCs. Maybe when we level up enough, a bridge will open and you'll be able to go back to Los Espíritus," said Claire.

"You're forgetting this game was banned the day it was released. We stole the only copy from the National Library of Scotland. Nobody is working on DLCs."

"And even if we could get to Los Espíritus, we would still be in the fifties. None of the stuff we have in TDA Online will be there. No yacht, no submarine, no penthouse apartments, no stilt houses, no aircraft, no garage full of supercars, no arcade."

No arcade! The enormity of what he had done began to dawn on Milton.

Epilogue

London February 19 2047.

At 9am precisely two perfectly groomed footmen wearing tailcoats and white kid gloves strode across the courtyard of Buckingham Palace. One of them was carrying an ornate gilded easel and the second a framed document. They stopped in front of the main gates, unfolded the easel and set the document carefully upon it. Then they stood back and took a minute to check their work: the frame was precisely centered on the easel and the easel was placed exactly parallel to the palace railing and sufficiently close to be easily read by a commoner in the street. Satisfied they turned and marched back to the servants entrance of the palace. A curtain twitched briefly in a first floor apartment as the Queen looked out in satisfaction at the proceedings.

Outside in the street an intern from The Thunderer, the sole member of the press despatched to cover the event, aligned the lens of her camera with a gap in the railings and zoomed in on the announcement on the easel.

"The Queen and the Royal Family are delighted at the news that Her Royal Highness Princess Mathilda was safely delivered of a daughter at 3.23am today. Her Royal Highness and her child are both doing well."

Author's Note

Dear Reader,

Thank you for reading 'The Repository Suppository'. I hope you enjoyed it as much as I enjoyed writing it!

During the Covid lockdowns I spent a lot of time playing Grand Theft Auto. The game world and my character's little corner of it - a two bedroom apartment in Grapeseed opposite an amusement arcade - was an escape for me to somewhere without masks and curfews. I'd like to thank all the developers at RockStar for creating the most compelling simulated worlds yet achieved. Other companies and researchers talk pretentiously about the metaverse but GTA and Red Dead Online with their outstanding maps and immersion have come closest to making it real. Like everyone else, I'm waiting impatiently for GTA 6 and expecting great things.

More Future Edinburgh books are planned. There is already an early draft of the next one, the last few years have given plenty of fuel for the political satire fire.

Keep up with the series on Twitter @rassleigh or Facebook https://www.facebook.com/sean.t.rassleigh

All the best,

Sean.

P.S. If you enjoyed the book, I'd really appreciate it if you could leave a review!

Printed in Great Britain
by Amazon